Webster

Tale of an Outlaw

Webster

Tale of an Outlaw

Ellen Emerson White

Aladdin

NEW YORK   LONDON   TORONTO   SYDNEY   NEW DELHI

ALADDIN

An imprint of Simon & Schuster Children's Publishing Division

1230 Avenue of the Americas, New York, New York 10020

First Aladdin hardcover edition November 2015

Text copyright © 2015 by Ellen Emerson White

Jacket illustration copyright © 2015 by Petra Brown

All rights reserved, including the right of reproduction in whole or in part in any form.

ALADDIN is a trademark of Simon & Schuster, Inc., and related logo is a registered trademark of Simon & Schuster, Inc.

For information about special discounts for bulk purchases, please contact Simon & Schuster Special Sales at 1-866-506-1949 or business@simonandschuster.com.

The Simon & Schuster Speakers Bureau can bring authors to your live event. For more information or to book an event contact the Simon & Schuster Speakers Bureau at 1-866-248-3049 or visit our website at www.simonspeakers.com.

Jacket designed by Karina Granda

Interior designed by Hilary Zarycky

The text of this book was set in ITC New Baskerville.

Manufactured in the United States of America 1015 FFG

2 4 6 8 10 9 7 5 3 1

Library of Congress Cataloging-in-Publication Data

White, Ellen Emerson.

Webster : tale of an outlaw / by Ellen Emerson White. —First Aladdin hardcover edition.

—pages cm

Summary: When Webster the dog arrives at Green Meadows Farm he has already been adopted, mistreated, and given away three times and is done with people, but the other animals of the shelter will not let him give up on the possibility of a special family.

ISBN 978-1-4814-2201-7 (hc)

[1. Dogs—Fiction. 2. Animal shelters—Fiction. 3. Cats—Fiction. 4. Animals—Treatment—Fiction.] I. Title.

PZ7.W58274Web 2015

[FIC]—dc23

2014049261

ISBN 978-1-14814-2203-1 (eBook)

For Donna, who cared for the real *Bad Hat for so long, before bringing him into my life, and for Estelle, who is very fond of Harold*

Webster
Tale of an Outlaw

CHAPTER ONE

The dog was way too cool to be scared. Or alarmed. Or even a tiny bit *nervous*.

But, apparently, when it came to being adopted, the third time *wasn't* the charm.

Did he care? Nope. Whatever was going to happen, was going to happen—even if it was bad. No big deal. He could handle it.

Probably.

He had been so happy when the big, noisy family adopted him—but, he probably should have known that it wasn't going to work out when the first two things they did were to slap a tight, metal-pronged choke collar around his neck, and then name him "Beast."

It also maybe hadn't been a good sign that they left

him outside every single night, chained to a rusty metal fence. Even when it was cold, or raining—or *snowing*, he would be stuck out there by himself, trying not to shiver.

Today, one of the little girls in the family had snuck him into the kitchen, even though he was supposed to stay in the yard on his chain. She'd tried to dry off his fur with some paper towels, and then put a bowl of cereal on the floor for him to eat. Cornflakes and milk weren't exactly his favorites, but the dog was so hungry that he pretty much *inhaled* them.

Then, the father came into the room and tripped over him. He yelled, "Bad dog!" and kicked him as hard as he could in the ribs. The dog had tried to scramble out of the way—and the man kicked him again, even harder. There was a lot of yelling and commotion, the kids started crying—from the baby, all the way up to the thirteen-year-old boy.

At that point, the mother slammed a plate down on the counter so hard that it broke. "That's it, I can't take it anymore!" she shouted. "He goes *now!*"

The next thing the dog knew, the father stomped off to work, and the rest of the family got in the car. The kids were all still crying, and begging for another chance, and promising to take better care of their Beast—but, the mother didn't seem to be listening.

They took him to an animal hospital first, to try to have him "put to sleep"—which were possibly the three worst words in the whole world. Luckily, the veterinarians had refused to do it, and the family ended up bringing him to a place called the Green Meadows Rescue Group, instead. It seemed to be a farm, and there was a big white house with freshly painted black shutters, and an old red barn, and lots of outdoor kennels and fields. A few people were carrying around hoses and buckets and that sort of thing, and a bunch of dogs were running in a big grassy area, enclosed by a tall wooden fence. He could smell lots of dogs and cats, along with some horses and geese and chickens, and what might be a goat, too.

The children were all still really upset, but the mean mother signed some papers, and handed him over to a lady named Joan, who was the owner of the shelter or something. And then, just like that, the family piled back into their car and drove away. *Left* him. Alone.

The dog watched anxiously until the car was gone. Maybe they would change their minds, and come back? Not that it had been a great home, but at least he had *had* a home. His throat felt tight, and he was having trouble swallowing. With luck, no one would be able to tell how afraid he was.

Because, okay, he *was* scared. Petrified, even.

Joan reached down to pat him. She had long brown hair pulled back into a thick ponytail, and was wearing hiking boots, jeans, and a green sweatshirt with the black silhouette of a running dog on the front of it. "It's okay, buddy," she said, in a very kind voice. "You're going to be fine now."

The dog had learned a long time ago not to trust people—and he wasn't about to start now. He could hear some barking out in the meadow, but it didn't sound frightened, or frantic. So maybe, as shelters went, this was a fairly nice one? Maybe he wouldn't be shivering on a wet, filthy cement floor for weeks on end this time? He hoped so, anyway.

A tall man with glasses and a lot of unruly blondish hair came out of the house, walking an arrogant little Yorkshire Terrier on a leash.

"What do we have here?" the man asked.

Joan sighed. "That family just gave him to us. Look at how thin the poor thing is."

The man nodded. "It looks like he hasn't had a decent meal in *weeks*."

Okay, the dog would admit that he was rather slim, but in a totally excellent *athletic* sort of way.

In the meantime, the Terrier gave him a cocky *You think you're tough? I'm tough!* look.

Which the dog chose to ignore.

"I run this joint," the Terrier barked at him.

Oh, yeah, no doubt. "Move along, buddy," the dog barked back. "Nothing to see here."

The Terrier laughed. "You've got *that* right," he said in a high yap.

The dog had walked into that one—so, he couldn't be offended by the insult.

Much.

The dog tugged experimentally on the leash, and felt the metal prongs bite into his neck. He *hated* this collar. If this Joan person took it off him soon, he might actually start to like her.

A little.

Maybe.

"*Touch* any of my toys, and I will vanquish you," the Yorkshire Terrier muttered.

Yeah, right. "You and what munchkin-dog army, little man?" the dog asked.

"Okay, guys, calm down," Joan said, with a laugh. "You don't need to bark at him, Jack." Which was obviously the Terrier's name.

The Terrier gave the dog a long *do* not *underestimate me* blink—and the dog resisted the urge to step on him.

Joan was talking to the man, who seemed to be named Thomas, about taking him to the vet—*whoa!*—but then, another shelter worker came out of the house and told her that the vet, Dr. Kasanofsky, was going to drive over as soon as his office hours were finished and examine him right here, instead.

As far as the dog was concerned, that was strike one for life on the rescue farm.

Joan led him inside, where there was a small office near the front door. File cabinets, desks, computers, and other boring stuff. It looked like the area off to the right was a regular house, and that the newer wing on the left was for animals. When the dog had been in other shelters, there were stained concrete floors everywhere, dented metal dishes full of stale water, and lots of rusty chain link fencing. With luck, this place wasn't going to be as awful as those had been.

Not that he was planning to stay long. In fact, the first chance he got, he was going to escape. He was *done* with people. He would hit the open road soon enough, off to a new life of adventure, excitement, and, like, *hijinks!*

There seemed to be a couple of rooms set aside just for cats—not his favorite animals, so that was strike *two*— with lots of pillows on the floor, and carpeted climbing structures. Maybe the cats had their own cages, too, but he couldn't see any.

They passed a grooming and bathing room, what looked like a doctor's office, and a big kitchen. The kitchen smelled good, and he could see an older woman putting some large flat metal sheets into an oven.

"Do you have anything special for our new friend here, Monica?" Joan asked.

The older woman smiled. "Oh, isn't he a beauty! What's his name?"

She thought he was beautiful. Okay, in that case, despite his intense dislike of all human beings, the dog already kind of dug Monica.

And, you know, she was *right*. He was nothing if not devilishly handsome.

"His owners were calling him *Beast*," Joan said.

"Oh, how awful. We'll have to come up with something better than that." Monica reached into a wicker basket, which seemed to be full of freshly baked dog biscuits. "Here you go, pal," she said, and held one out to the dog.

He could smell liver and garlic and many other pleasant things. And the biscuit was still slightly warm! His stomach hurt a lot, and he really didn't feel like eating, but he held the biscuit in his mouth, in case he changed his mind. He had never had a homemade biscuit before, and the concept sort of blew his mind, to be honest.

The dog area was a long corridor lined with small, indoor rooms, which were equipped with beds with canvas or fleece covers. The dog expected to be thrown into one of the kennels and ignored, but instead, Joan brought him into a room with low couches and thick rugs. There were balls and rawhide bones and Kong toys lying all over the floor, and he stared at them in confusion.

Although if he could figure out which ones belonged to the cocky Yorkshire Terrier, he would be tempted to chew each of them just enough to be annoying.

Joan unsnapped his leash, and the dog quickly looked around, to see if there was an easy escape route.

The two windows had screens, and he could probably leap through them—but, the openings were kind of narrow, and maybe he would bide his time.

At least until he found the energy to eat his biscuit, because it would be just plain *wrong* to let it go to waste.

He was startled when she took off his collar, and slipped a soft red nylon one over his head, instead. But, it felt a lot better around his neck, no question about that.

He wasn't sure what he was supposed to do, so he stood stiffly by the door, waiting to see what was going to happen next.

Joan sat down on one of the throw rugs, folded her arms around her knees, and watched him for a minute. "You've had a tough time, haven't you, fella," she said finally.

Well, yeah, maybe he had, but the dog didn't necessarily think of it that way. He was an admirably strong survivor, and maybe even a role model for canine fortitude—not some pathetic victim.

And proud *of* it.

After a while, she came over and patted him—which he permitted, but didn't encourage.

"Okay, no pressure," she said, and withdrew.

Thomas came in to tell her that the vet had arrived. So, Joan brought him down to the room that looked like a medical office, and the dog slowly stepped onto a clean metal table that felt slippery under his paws. When it started to rise into the air, he almost jumped off, but Joan gave him a soothing pat.

"Don't worry, it's okay," she said. She squinted at the number on the tiny screen above the table. "Seventy-three pounds! You're going to be big, once you gain enough weight to be healthy."

Too big, the mean family had always said.

The veterinarian walked into the room with a small medical bag. He was a cheerful-looking guy, with curly hair and a mustache.

"Thank you so much for coming over here, Dr. K.," Joan said. "He's pretty stressed out."

What, was that surprising, under the circumstances? Yeah, he was much cooler than the average dog—cooler than *any* other dog, in fact—but, that didn't mean that he wasn't a nervous wreck, at the moment.

"Well, I can certainly understand why he would be. Hey, there," Dr. K. said to him, and held out the back of his hand.

Since it seemed like the sensible thing to do, the dog dutifully sniffed the vet's hand.

"Don't worry, boy," Dr. K. said. "We'll take our time, and make this as easy as possible."

The dog had his temperature taken—which was no fun. Then, Dr. K. began the full exam, checking his eyes and ears and teeth first.

The dog *wanted* to pull away from him, but made a point of trying to stay detached, instead. Let them do whatever terrible things they were going to do to him, and just not pay much attention, if possible. Besides, it was always better if people thought that animals had no idea what they were saying.

"What do you know about him?" Dr. K. asked.

"Not much, although I think he may have come from a shelter somewhere here in New Hampshire," Joan said. "The mother said they had had him for a few months, but that he was too difficult for them to handle."

Dr. K. shook his head, as he checked the dog's legs, hips and paws. "He seems pretty gentle to me."

"Once he relaxes, I think he's going to be an absolute sweetie pie," Joan said.

Was that what she thought? The dog was entirely

confident that she was wrong about that. She would be lucky if he decided to be nothing more than *ornery*, as opposed to outright surly or hostile. But, he could pretty well guarantee that "sweet" was never going to happen. Not no way, not no how.

"I'm guessing he's mostly Labrador retriever," Joan said, "but what else do you think is in the mix?"

Dr. K. studied the dog carefully. "With the red under-coat, maybe some Rhodesian Ridgeback? Or possibly even Vizsla or Redbone Coonhound."

Okay, now they were *both* very much mistaken. He was a black dog—*all* black, and totally fierce and independent and impressive. In fact, he was his own special breed, which could never be duplicated.

Just, you know, for the record.

"He's certainly favoring his right side," Dr. K. said.

They could *tell*? The dog instantly stood up straighter, even though it hurt. A lot.

"The mother said he was climbing around and fell off their swing set and might have gotten 'banged up.' Had they ever brought him in for an exam?" Joan asked.

"No," Dr. K. said. "They showed up out of the blue for the first time today, and she said they wanted to have him put to sleep. So, when they wouldn't surrender him to us, we sent them over here to you, instead. I had Jeff drive over behind them, to make sure that they didn't just let him loose somewhere."

Really? Okay, the dog hadn't even noticed that. He needed to work on his spy skills.

Joan looked disgusted. "Can you imagine? A wonderful, healthy dog like this? What's the matter with people?"

Dr. K. shrugged, putting his stethoscope in his ears. "I'm afraid I had to stop asking myself that a long time ago."

When the vet started palpating his ribs, the dog winced in spite of himself, because it hurt so much.

"I'm sorry," Dr. K. said, and instantly lessened the pressure. He frowned, and checked inside the dog's mouth again—although the dog couldn't imagine why. Then, he felt the dog's ribs some more, and checked his heart, stomach, liver, and kidneys.

"What do you think?" Joan asked.

"The same thing you do," Dr. K. said. "Someone kicked him, probably more than once. I don't think anything's broken, and there doesn't seem to be any internal bleeding, but I want to run some bloodwork and do a urinalysis. Heartworm test, vaccinations, the works. He's a little dehydrated, too, so I'd like to give him some fluids."

To the dog's absolute horror, he had to stay in the little medical office for a few hours, lying on a fluffy towel, with a needle taped to his front leg, and a big IV bag hanging above him. He was too tense even to close his eyes, so he just waited grimly for the treatment to be over.

When the IV bag was finally empty, and Dr. K. patted him and left, Joan put a rabies tag on his nylon collar, and gave him a new name: Webster.

Webster. Hmmm. It sounded pretty smart, but he wasn't crazy about it. Although it was a lot better than "Beast." But, whatever. For now, apparently, he was Webster. Not that it mattered. He wasn't planning to answer to it, anyway.

Joan brought him back down the long hallway, and set him up in a small wooden room, with redbrick–patterned linoleum on the floor, and a soft fleece bed for sleeping on. It was a kennel, although he had to admit that it was a lot nicer than any of the ones he had ever been in before. But, prison was still prison.

There was a low swinging door on the other side of the room, so he could go outside to go to the bathroom anytime he wanted. Not that he had the energy to go check it out. Yeah, he was still going to escape and have adventures and everything—but, maybe he would wait until tomorrow, when he was less tired.

From what he could see through the opening, the door led to a fenced-in concrete run. He was curious about what would happen if he had an accident on the floor—would they yell and scream at him, and call him a Beast? Probably, yeah.

There were other dogs in the kennels next to his, and even more dogs in the kennels across the hall, but he didn't care enough to go to the door and check to see who his new neighbors were. What did it matter? It wasn't like they were going to be friends, or anything. They were just like, *cell mates.*

There was a big sturdy bowl full of cool, fresh water in his kennel, and a dish with some hard brown kernels in it. They smelled much better than the ones he had usually been given, but he still wasn't hungry. So, he just sniffed at the food, took a small drink of water, and then stood by the wall.

"It's okay, Webster," Joan said, and indicated the fleece bed. "You can lie down right here."

Maybe later. When he was alone.

As suppertime approached, the atmosphere around the farm seemed to get louder and more excited. All of the other animals were eager to have their evening meals, apparently, and there was a lot of barking and meowing going on. Monica, the elderly lady who had baked the dog biscuits, brought him a dish filled with cooked hamburger, hard-boiled eggs, mashed carrots, brown rice, and other stuff. It smelled good, and even though he was exhausted, he took a couple of bites. Then, aware that she was watching him intently, he retreated and stood by the wall again.

"Oh, you poor thing," she said. "Don't you worry, Webster dear, soon you'll be feeling nice and strong."

Maybe. He waited until she was gone, and then he took two more bites. But, that was enough effort to make him feel tired again. He stretched out on the floor instead, moving carefully so that he didn't jar his ribs.

People kept coming to check on him, and he would wake up for a few seconds, and then go back to sleep. To his shock, later that night, Joan brought in a sleeping bag and slept on the floor right next to him. It made the dog uncomfortable, but he had to admit that it was nice to know that someone was concerned about how he was doing. He couldn't ever remember having anything like that happen before.

He spent the next day sitting either on the linoleum, or on the cement in the outdoor run. But, when he was outside, the dogs on either side of him—including the irritating Yorkshire Terrier—kept trying to talk to him, and be friendly, and all—and he just wasn't into it. Not even a little bit. So, for the most part, he stayed inside, where he could have some privacy.

At about noon, Monica carried in an early lunch of plain chicken, rice, and yoghurt, but he still couldn't quite bring himself to finish the entire dish of food. Partially because his stomach still hurt, but also because the simple truth was that he really didn't have any appetite, because he was sad. Very, very sad.

Maybe the family that had adopted him hadn't been nice, but it was pretty mind-blowing to get *returned* to a shelter, like a shirt that didn't fit, or something. It made him feel small. And damaged.

Which was really depressing.

It was creepy to have people peeking in at him all the time, so he got up, pushed through the swinging door, and went out to his cement run for a while. The dog in the cage on his left tried talking to him again, but he pretended he didn't hear him, and stared blankly out at the farm. It was kind of cold, but he liked being in the fresh air. In fact, he liked it so much that even when it started raining, he stayed outside.

Later, when Monica brought his dinner in, he quickly gulped down half of it, so that everyone would stop *hovering* over him already. Then, he went back outside and curled up on the wet cement.

The next time he woke up, it was dark. The rain was still coming down, and he was completely soaked. Would he get in trouble if he came inside and got the kennel all wet? Maybe. So, it was probably safer to stay outdoors and let the rain keep falling on him.

On the other hand, it was very quiet, and maybe all of the people and other animals had gone to bed. So, it might be okay to go inside and lie down on the floor. In fact, if no one was looking, he might even finally try out that tempting-looking fleece bed.

So, the dog hauled himself up from the cement and

shook off as much water as he could. Then, he ducked through the swinging door and went inside. Yes! The lights were out everywhere, and he was by himself! Excellent.

The dog immediately flopped down on the bed, and was delighted to find out how comfortable it was. Wow, he had wasted a lot of time out there on the soggy cement, when he could have been resting in here, instead. When the people got up in the morning and started looking at him, he could always go back outside, if he felt like it.

With everyone keeping such a close eye on him, he hadn't seen anything *resembling* an opportunity to run away. So, he would just have to be patient, and bide his time. Then, when the moment arrived—*whoosh!* Off he would go, never to return.

And since he wasn't sticking around, he couldn't think of any good reasons to try and be cooperative and fit in. He was a bad dog, right? That was the rumor, anyway. And bad dogs totally were not team players.

So, okay. He could make his own rules, and be a proud, noble dog that everyone would admire, but never quite understand. He would never depend on anyone again, and no one would ever have a chance to be mean to him. He could picture himself strutting down the street, while people watched eagerly and wished that he would to choose to live with *them*—not the other way around.

Yep, that was his plan. He would be a loner. A rebel. A canine *icon*. They would write inspiring songs and poems in his honor, he would trend all over the Internet, and Hollywood would film unforgettable action movies about him, that did *huge* box office during their opening weekends.

Oh, yeah, that would be awesome.

But, he was going to need a much better name than *Webster*. It would be hard to be an icon, if he didn't have a really impressive name. Something memorable, and dashing. A name to create fear and awe in the hearts of all who were lucky enough to pass his way.

He drifted off to sleep, dreaming about what the journey towards being a canine celebrity would be like. Then, right in the middle of an entertaining part about him being the supreme commander of a pack of admiring and respectful dogs, his eyes flew open.

What was *that?*

Somewhere, out in the corridor, he could hear a

strange, scary sound. Was it—stomping? No, it was more like something *stumping* along. Stumping, and skittering, and—he had never heard anything like it.

And whatever it was, it sounded like it was headed straight towards him!

CHAPTER TWO

The dog scrabbled into the back of his kennel, hoping that the monster wouldn't notice him in the dark. Luckily, he hadn't once been named Shadow—by the crummy owners he had had *before* the mean family—because he was easy to see. He was too big and tough to be afraid of anything, but— well—monsters were different. Monsters were scary.

Stump, stump, skitter, skitter, stump.

What *was* it? Only something extremely dangerous would make eerie noises like that. Okay, it was maybe a *small* monster, but he knew for sure that it was a monster.

Then, he heard an even worse noise—*something was rattling at the latch on his kennel door.*

Okay, okay. Time to remember that he was a very

fearsome, large dog. Maybe the monster would be afraid of *him*? In fact, if the monster dared to come inside, he would show his teeth, growl fiercely, and then attack it.

Or, um, maybe slink past it, and run to safety?

There was a clank, and then slowly—ever so slowly, *terrifyingly* slowly—the door swung open.

Okay. This was it. The dog took a deep breath and promised himself that he would be brave, and go down fighting. He would make sure that the monster would remember that he had tangled with a *true* beast.

Stump, skitter, stump, skitter. Then, he heard little erratic claws scraping across the floor, and—the monster was standing right in front of him! It had big crooked yellow eyes, and long talons, and—oh.

It was a cat. A weird-looking, tiny—but frightening— cat, with slightly crossed eyes and a big black splotch across its white face, like a defective mustache.

Then again, lots of times, cats were untrustworthy and vicious, right? And violent? So, the dog waited, tensely, to see what was going to happen.

"Hello," the cat said. "I am Florence."

Wait, the cat had a British accent. What was up with that?

"It's all right," the cat said. "Joan and Thomas are upstairs asleep, and it's after midnight."

Even so, the dog just stared at her.

"Please tell me you know how to talk," Florence said. "It will be most unsettling, otherwise."

Of course he could talk. He just didn't, very often. Since he had lost his family many months ago, back in Arkansas, his encounters with other animals had usually been brief, and raising his fur or wagging his tail or whatever had been enough.

"*Well?*" the cat said, looking impatient.

"Why do you have a British accent?" he asked.

It was quiet for a few seconds.

"Because I can," Florence said grandly.

The dog blinked, forgot how aloof he was—and laughed. She might be a cat, but there was still something plucky and hilarious about her.

"Everyone's very worried," Florence said. "I heard them saying that you're barely eating, and that you've mostly just been lying here staring at nothing for hours on end."

Yeah. So? The dog didn't say anything. Or move.

"Planning on getting up anytime soon?" Florence asked.

Nope. He was not.

"Well, I simply won't have it," Florence said, and stamped one of her paws on the floor for emphasis. "There's been quite enough moping, and you will come with me *right now*."

The dog started to jump to his feet, but then paused. "I don't want to," he said. "And I'm a very, *very* bad dog, missy, so don't try to argue with me."

Florence sighed. "You dogs take rejection so hard— it's awfully tedious. Now, come along. We have kibble and biscuits."

They had food? Okay. He was extremely wicked and all—but, he was also hungry, and besides, she sounded like she meant business.

She led him down the dark hallway, and he could see that a few of the dogs were sleeping, while other cage doors were open.

"Do you pick and choose who gets to come out at night?" the dog whispered.

Florence shook her head. "Some of them are going to the adoption fair tomorrow in town, so they're resting up. Put their best feet forward and such."

The dog wasn't sure what an adoption fair was, but

Florence was stumping so briskly and efficiently down the hall that he was afraid to interrupt her again. Her walk was a strange limping stagger, and as he trotted behind her, he tried to pretend that he hadn't noticed.

"I have no cerebellum," Florence said.

The dog nodded uneasily.

"Dr. K. thinks that my mother maybe had distemper when I was born, and so, my brain didn't form properly, and my balance is a bit dodgy." Florence paused. "Also, I got hit by a car."

Well, that could do it, yeah.

"And I'm diabetic," Florence said. "So, I'm unadoptable."

The dog noticed that she had only a tiny little stub of a tail, too, but maybe that had happened in the accident with the car. He decided not to mention it, in case it brought back bad memories.

"However," Florence said, "you will be happy to know that I have no cognitive impairments whatsoever." She glanced up at him, and immediately lost her balance and fell over—but then, rolled back up onto her feet. "Well? Are you happy to hear about that?"

"Um, yes, ma'am," he said politely. "That's surely good news. Congratulations."

She nodded. "Which is as it should be. You are Webster, correct?"

"For now," the dog said. Until he escaped, anyway. "I don't really like it."

"They do their best," Florence said. "We have so many animals come through here, that I think they've run out of names. And Webster is dignified." She squinted at him with her little crossed eyes. "Although it is not clear to me whether *you* are dignified. We shall have to see."

The dog followed her to the room with the low couches and brightly colored rugs. To his surprise, the den was full of dogs and cats lounging around. It looked almost like they were having a party.

"This is Webster-Until-He-Gets-A-Better-Name," Florence announced. "Be sweet to him—he's still deeply mired in his traumatized phase."

The animals all nodded sympathetic nods.

The room was so crowded that the dog hung back near the door, feeling shy.

"Well, come on now," Florence said. "Spit spot!"

Spit spot?

"Hey there, Grumpy!" a voice yelled, and he saw the mouthy Yorkshire Terrier over on one of the couches.

Okay, at least he knew someone in the room. Sort of. The dog gave him a brief nod.

"That's Jack," Florence said. "He's been here for about four months."

"*Everybody* wants to adopt me," Jack said proudly. "But, I'm very choosy, and won't go with just anyone."

Another dog, who was a Border Collie mix, laughed. "He's really loud. Nobody's taking that little yapper home."

From his place on the couch, Jack looked crushed.

"MacNulty," Florence said in a warning voice.

"Sorry, man," the Border Collie said quickly. "Everyone knows you're probably the cutest one here—you'll definitely have a new family before any of the rest of us do."

Jack brightened when he heard that. "That's right! And when it happens, I'll be sitting pretty."

Florence introduced the dog to an elderly female Bernese Mountain Dog mix named Pico, a black cat with white markings named Bert—who had his mouth stuffed with kibble, and a sly-looking tortoiseshell cat named Kerry. The dog knew he would never remember all of the names, but he nodded at each one of them in turn.

MacNulty, the Border Collie mix, seemed to have a lot of restless energy and kept shifting his weight from one paw to the other, and jumping in place every so often.

Border Collies were *so* predictable. "Looking for something to herd?" the dog asked.

MacNulty nodded. "You bet! I figure I'll get adopted by some farmers and get to herd *all day long*. It's going to be great!"

Well, okay, whatever. The dog thought it was strange that, apparently, they all not only expected to be adopted, but that they *wanted* it to happen. He, for one, had no interest in having strangers take him away ever again.

Florence waved one of her palsied little paws at a hulking German Shepherd who was taking up half of a couch. "And that's Duke."

"I used to be King," the German Shepherd said. "But, I got downgraded."

The dog laughed—but then, realized that the shepherd wasn't kidding. "Oh. Sorry to hear that."

Duke shrugged amiably. "You never know. I might work my way back up."

"And that is Lancelot," Florence said, indicating a shaggy Afghan Hound mix.

Lancelot gave him a nod. "Dude," he said, in a surfer's drawl.

"That's Matthew, up on the shelf," Florence said, pointing at a scruffy old black cat who was perched on a bookcase.

"Don't take it personally, if I bite you," Matthew said, and showed his teeth. Lots of teeth. "I'm still kind of feral."

Okay, good to know. The dog nodded—and kept his distance.

From a well-padded easy chair, a sleek Seal Point Siamese cat looked at the dog suspiciously. "I'm Benjamin, and I'm from the city. The *big* city. Do you have a problem with that?"

What? "No," the dog said. "Should I?"

"You should *not*," Benjamin said.

Well, all right. The dog shrugged. "Okay. Then, I don't."

Benjamin narrowed his eyes. "You hesitated. It sounded like you hesitated." He turned to Florence. "I don't like him. Send him away!"

"You certainly enjoy the sound of your own voice," Florence said wryly.

Benjamin smiled a wide smile. "Yes, I think it has a

very pleasant timbre. Thank you for noticing."

The dog was starting to wonder whether these were the animals who had gotten *turned down* by the Island of Misfit Toys.

"Food," Bert, the black-and-white cat, said, staring miserably down at his empty dish. "I need more food." He sighed, hauled himself up onto all four paws, and then stuck his head inside a large bag of kibble.

For a minute or so, the only sound in the room was Bert crunching noisily.

"Well, then," Florence said. "Moving on now."

He met several other dogs and cats, but it was hard to keep track of everyone's names, especially since he wasn't exactly Mr. Social. So, the dog just nodded and shrugged, and that sort of thing. It wasn't like he was planning to be pals with anyone.

"What's your story, Webster?" Cole, a stolid grey cat, asked.

What, was he supposed to tell his sad tale, and *emote*, and all? Not likely. The dog shrugged. "This is my fourth shelter." Or fifth? It was hard to keep track. "I've pretty much had it. And I don't like the name Webster, either. I'm going to need something a whole lot cooler than that."

"Well, maybe the people who adopt you next will think of a name you like better," MacNulty said.

Oh, yeah, right. "No one's going to want me," the dog said. Not that he wanted *them*, either. "I do terrible things."

Jack sat up, looking intrigued. "Like what?"

The dog had never quite figured that out, so he shrugged.

"I think that the people were probably not nice, and that it has nothing to do with you," Kerry said.

Maybe. "The first time I had a home, I ate cardboard one day," the dog said. "The part from inside a roll of paper towels. That really bothered them."

Duke's eyes brightened. "Cardboard is *good*. Cardboard is *really* good. I love cardboard!"

The other dogs nodded happily, while the cats all exchanged glances.

"If you're not careful, Duke," Florence said, "you're going to be bumped down to Earl."

Duke looked horrified. "I don't want that to happen. How low could I go?"

"No name at all," Benjamin said, without hesitating. "We would just call you Dog or It."

Duke shuddered. "I better be careful, then. Try not to screw up anymore."

Did he really not know that cats made dire threats, purely for their own amusement, not because they had actual *power?* "They're cats, man," the dog said. "If they call you a name you don't like, just don't answer to it."

Duke's eyes widened even more. "I couldn't do that. I'm a dog. We answer to our names. *Always.*"

Well, on Duke's planet, maybe.

"He's right, Webster," Florence said.

The dog automatically looked over at her.

Florence laughed. "See? You did it yourself."

He hadn't answered to it. He had just been—polite. "Well, all I know for sure is that I don't want to be adopted again," the dog said. "Ever."

Every single other animal in the room gasped.

"*Everyone* wants to be adopted," Matthew, the scruffy black cat, said. "I'm not even friendly—and I still want my own special family."

Okay, so then he would be the exception who proved the rule. "Nope. Not me. Been there, done that, tired of getting kicked around," the dog said.

Literally and figuratively.

"But, the next people might be nice," Cole said.

Yeah. Sure. The dog wasn't going to hold his breath about that. "Nope, I'm done," he said. "Been adopted.

Three times. Didn't like it. First chance I get, I'm going to escape from here, and make my own way in the world."

"You can't do that," Florence said. "Joan and Thomas would be very upset."

That was too bad and all, but not really his problem.

"What I want, more than anything, is for all of you to find happy homes," Florence said. "Of course, I'm unadoptable, because of my medical issues, but that isn't true for the rest of you. So, Webster, if you can, you really need to try and find a more positive attitude."

"Florence, I thought the reason you were unadoptable is because you're such an unbelievable cranky-pants," Benjamin said.

Florence nodded regally. "Yes, that, too."

The dog might have been in a bad mood, but he still almost laughed at that particular exchange.

"Lots of us have sad stories," Lancelot said. "That's just the way it rolls. But now that we're here, at the rescue group, we're all going to have happy endings. So, get with the program, dude."

How could a bunch of stray animals be so innocent and naive? The dog wasn't going to rain on their parades or anything, but they really didn't have a clue about the way things worked. "It's not *my* program," the dog said. "I want to go out there, and make a name for myself. And be really famous, because I'll be, you know, so totally dangerous and diabolical." Or—something like that. Really, his main motivation was to have adventures, and to have *fun*—and not to have any human beings ever tell him what to do.

The other animals mostly looked puzzled by this.

Pico, the elderly Bernese Mountain Dog mix, gave him a disapproving frown. "You, young retriever, are what my grandmother would have called a bad hat."

The dog had never heard that phrase before, but he was definitely intrigued. "What's a bad hat?"

"Everything a respectable animal does *not* want to be," Pico said.

Okay, that was pretty vague. "What do you mean? You have to be a little more clear," the dog said.

Pico frowned. "It doesn't really have a specific definition, Webster. It's a *concept*."

There was nothing at all clear about that. Did he look well-educated, or something? The dog tilted his head in confusion.

"Goodness, what a bother," Pico said impatiently. "A

bad hat is someone who is a troublemaker. A ne'er-do-well. Unruly. Obnoxious."

Well, those were all words the dog liked very much. "So far, so good," he said. "What else?"

"I don't know. It's just—*badness*," Pico said, and looked at the other animals for help.

"Disreputable," Florence said. "Dissolute. *Difficult.*"

This was just getting better and better. "And?" the dog asked eagerly.

"Obstreperous," Benjamin said. "Rebellious. Untrustworthy. Entirely unwelcome in every way, shape, or form in polite society."

Wow, that sounded totally awesome. The dog glanced around the room, hoping that someone else would have a contribution.

"Bad," Lancelot said finally, and everyone else nodded. "Wicked bad."

Talk about excellent! "You mean like a villain, and an outlaw, and someone who strikes fear into the hearts of all who pass?" the dog asked.

Pico nodded, pursing her lips in disgust. "A hooligan, also."

A bad hat. Cool! "I *love* it," the dog said. "That's just

what I am. Except, I don't want to be *a* bad hat. I want to be *the* Bad Hat." The *best* Bad Hat.

"I think you're missing the point, Webster," Florence said. "It wasn't a compliment."

Maybe not to wimpy cats, or to timid and unimaginative sorts of dogs, but as far as he was concerned, it was just right. "It's *perfect,*" the dog said. "Finally, a name that I can enjoy. Thanks, Pico!"

Now and forever, no matter what, until the end of time, he would be—the Bad Hat!

CHAPTER THREE

Benjamin was the first one to break the silence.

"You invited him here, Miss Cranky-Pants," he said to Florence. "All of this is on your head."

"Let's just start, before it gets light out," MacNulty said impatiently. "Can we watch *Babe* again?"

"That'll do, MacNulty," Jack said, and laughed so hard that he almost fell off the couch.

Florence turned to look at the dog. "It's your first night, Bad Hat. What would you like to watch?"

What on earth was she talking about? The dog looked at her with confusion.

"It's a *viewing party*, dude," Lancelot said. "So, yo, big fella, that means we watch something."

Really? This wasn't just sitting around eating kibble and yapping at each other? There was an actual *plan*? "Uh, I don't know," the Bad Hat said. "I don't really watch TV."

The other animals in the room gasped.

"I've mostly been in shelters and stuff," the Bad Hat said, feeling very defensive. And it wasn't like he wasn't totally, sort of, up on his pop culture, since *all* animals were, which was one of the best secrets that human beings didn't know about them. But, was it his fault that he hadn't been around televisions much? Yeah, he'd *seen* televisions before, but mostly, all of his adopters had left him outside by himself. And if he was allowed in the house, he was usually supposed to stay in the kitchen. If he went into the bedrooms—or, worst of all, tried to climb up on the couch with the children or something, all he would hear was, "No, no, bad dog!" Then, he would get banished to the backyard again. In one of the shelters, the guy who was supposed to clean the kennels always sat and watched movies on his computer all day, and the dog would look out from his cage and try to follow along. The kennel guy watched sports, too, which the dog had enjoyed. A lot.

"Uh, whatever you guys want to watch is fine with me," he said.

Benjamin looked eager. "Shall we?"

Florence nodded decisively. "Yes. Let's show him our favorite. We'll watch the first episode, so he won't get lost."

At least five of the animals shouted, "Yay!" Then, they all settled into more comfortable positions and made sure that the food dishes were easy to reach.

They were so—congenial, and jolly. The Bad Hat didn't get it at all. But, he used his teeth to tug a bowl of kibble closer.

"Are there cowboys in it?" he asked. Because he liked cowboys a whole lot. Cowboys were his favorite.

They all shook their heads.

What? "I think I only like shows with cowboys," the Bad Hat said uneasily. "And scoundrels. And maybe some horses."

"There are a few horses," Jack said. "And a golden Retriever."

Kerry shook her head. "No, it's a yellow Lab."

"It's a golden Retriever!" Jack shouted. "I know it is!"

The other animals shook their heads, too.

"Oh," Jack said, and shrugged. "Well, okay, all I know is that it's some dog who looks dumb because he's too big, instead of being, you know, *compact*, like me."

"*Little*," MacNulty said, and Jack pretended not to hear him.

Well, if there was a dog, and some horses, the show might be okay. But, the Bad Hat would have preferred to see a whole bunch of cowboys. "Are there duels, and saloons, and frightened townspeople?" he asked.

The animals shook their heads.

Whoa, seriously? Maybe he should forget about this weird party, and go back to his kennel and get some sleep.

"Just watch," Florence said. "And enjoy snacks. But, *don't talk* while it's on. That's our one rule."

"And don't bite anyone," Matthew said. "Isn't that a rule, too?"

"It's a rule especially for *you*, Matt," Benjamin said.

"Okay." Matthew shrugged. "I knew it was a rule of some kind."

"So, it's all right if *I* bite anyone I want?" the Bad Hat asked, just to be difficult.

"*Shhh*," they all said.

Divas. He was surrounded by freakin' divas.

"Cole, if you please," Florence said to the big grey cat.

Cole nodded, and carefully tapped the buttons on various remote controls with his front paw, until the television was on, and a streaming video service appeared on the screen.

"He's our primary tech guy," Benjamin explained.

More weirdness. And the dog was much too cool to admit that he was impressed. But he was, since he didn't know how to work *any* electrical appliances, or even turn a doorknob without a lot of effort.

All of the animals' eyes were bright with anticipation. He had never seen a bunch of strays look so happy and content. Actually, he'd almost never really seen *anyone* looking happy and content.

Florence reached up and gave him a whack with her paw. "Please make some room for me, Bad Hat. It's much more secure for me to have a sturdy place to lean, when I'm on the couch."

What, she wanted to *lean* against him? Had he missed the part where he had said that would be okay?

"I, um, I sort of have boundary issues," the dog said. "So, maybe it would be better if—"

Never mind, she had already swung both paws up, and was hauling herself laboriously off the floor and onto the cushions. She lurched around to try and find her balance, and then fell on him—which didn't hurt, because she was tiny. But, it sure made him nervous. So, the dog held himself very rigidly, not sure what to do.

"It is not comfortable for me, if you sit like that," Florence said sternly.

When he'd woken up the other morning, he'd had a home, and a normal life. It maybe wasn't a great life, or a pleasant home, but he had gotten used to it. Now, he was living with a bunch of strangers, and a crippled *cat* was giving him instructions.

But, when she arranged herself against his shoulder, he let her do it, and tried to pretend that it didn't bother him.

"A dog pillow. *Excellent*," Bert, the cat who never seemed to stop eating, said through a mouth full of kibble. "Me, too!"

To the dog's dismay, the plump cat climbed right up onto his back, yawned, and stretched out. "Thanks, Bad Hat," Bert said sleepily. "Sometimes I have trouble staying awake during our shows, and I can have a good nap this way."

Great. He would have one cat on his shoulder, and another cat snoring on his back. It was so completely *not* what he would have expected to be doing tonight.

"We ready?" Cole asked.

"Play it, Sam," Benjamin said, and a collective little chuckle rippled among the animals.

When the opening theme for the show started playing, the Bad Hat was shocked that he recognized it.

"Wait, is that PBS?" he asked. "I don't watch PBS, no way."

"Shush," Florence said. "It's our favorite."

Oh, man, this was like one of his worst nightmares. Why couldn't he have ended up in a shelter where the animals watched normal stuff like football? And rooted loudly for the Razorbacks—as every sensible being should? "But, that sounds like *Masterpiece Classic*," the Bad Hat said. "Can I please go back to my kennel?"

Pico lifted her head to frown at him. "Mind your manners, Bad Hat. We look forward to this all day."

Great. What was next? Would they sit around doing algebra together? Baking cookies? Scrapbooking? Was this, like, an animal mental hospital? "But, *PBS*?" the dog said.

"Shhh!" about eight animals hissed in unison.

"You're gonna love it, dude," Lancelot said. "Kick back, and have some kibble."

Well, at least he liked kibble. The dog grumpily crunched some from the nearest dish.

"And don't be so fidgety," Florence said. "It disturbs my equilibrium."

Fine. Whatever. He was *definitely* going to have to figure out a way to escape from this crazy place.

Tonight, if possible.

The Bad Hat planned to hate every single second of the show—but, okay, he loved it. Immediately.

When the yellow Labrador Retriever made its first appearance, striding down the main staircase with some fancy guy, everyone cheered.

"Isis!" Bert said happily, stopping chewing for a second.

"Pharaoh," Benjamin corrected him. "Isis comes later."

"Pharaoh!" Bert said, just as happily.

Naturally, the yellow Lab was everyone's favorite character.

And even though he figured that he was losing outlaw coolness points by actually liking a show on public television, by the time they were halfway through the second episode, the Bad Hat was completely hooked. In fact, if he wasn't careful, he was going to end up wasting time wishing that someone would give him a PBS tote bag to treasure and chew on, or something.

Bert had fallen asleep almost immediately, but the dog was so caught up in the show, that he barely noticed the heavy weight on his back. In fact, when the rest of the animals decided to call it a night after the third episode, he was actually disappointed.

The cats all seemed to be very good with their paws, and had no trouble opening and closing the kennel doors. That way, it would look as though they had all spent the night sleeping peacefully on their donated pet beds— instead of sneaking out and having their viewing party. But, the Bad Hat felt a little embarrassed for the canine species, in general, when they had to have the cats stand up on their hind legs and flip the latches for them.

"So, are you still lonely and grouchy?" Florence asked, as Benjamin slapped the metal fastener on the dog's kennel into place, once he was inside.

Was he? The Bad Hat had to think about that. "Yes. But, maybe not as much as I was before."

"It's a start," Florence said. "Did you like the show?"

Well, the dog had a *little* pride left, so he couldn't admit that he had, um, maybe, possibly, enjoyed himself. "It was okay," he said. "But, it would have been much better if there were some cowboys in it."

Benjamin laughed. "Philistine," he said, and leaped over to Jack's door to close him in for the night, too.

The Bad Hat wasn't sure what that word meant—but, it didn't sound like a compliment.

"Not that I, you know, care or anything," he said, "but will we watch more episodes tomorrow night?"

Florence looked very amused. *"Absolutely,"* she said.

The animal shelter had a regular schedule every day. At about six thirty in the morning, all of the dogs started pacing around restlessly, waiting to go outside. Then, promptly at seven o'clock, Thomas and Joan came and brought them out to the big fenced-in meadow to run around.

For the first time, the dog was walked outside to join the others. Joan was watching him carefully—maybe to see if his ribs still hurt?—and he tried to make his gait look as effortless as possible. It must have worked, because she took his leash off, and patted him.

"Good boy," she said. "Have fun!"

Oh, yeah, he was *big* on fun. Famous for it.

But, it was great to be out of his kennel, and not on a leash. Maybe, finally, he would have his chance to escape? The Bad Hat stood near the gate, and looked around. The grass in the meadow was fairly long, and there were wildflowers growing all over the place—dandelions, daisies, and black-eyed Susans. Everyone was full of pent-up energy, so there was a lot of barking and chasing and running around in the grass. The dog ignored all of the rambunctious activity, even though part of him *ached* to join in, and run around like a goofball.

When he was a puppy, and he and his family had roamed the countryside in Arkansas, they'd always had such a great time. Sure, they were hungry sometimes, but he loved his mother, and his sisters and brother, and they were all very happy together.

Except, thinking about them broke his *most* serious rule. He missed them so much that he went out of his way not ever to wonder where they were, or worry about whether they were okay. The last time he had seen them was when the local dog officers showed up in a big truck, and tried to capture them. His sister bruised her paw on a rock, while they were running away, and they all stopped to help her. The dog wanted to protect his family, so when the officers came closer, he jumped in front of the other dogs, so that they could escape, and—nope. He *never* let himself think about this. Nope, nope, nope. It had been a long time ago, and he was really far away from them now, and there was nothing he could do to—all right, he would focus on something else, instead.

Like getting *away* from here, and starting his new life.

The Bad Hat took a couple of deep breaths, to clear his mind, and looked around some more. There was a tall wooden fence enclosing the entire meadow, which seemed to be pretty secure. He leaned against it experimentally, and gave the boards a hard shove with his shoulder. Which hurt, because the fence was sturdy, and very solid.

Well, okay, he wasn't going to be able to ram his way through it. Maybe there was a good place where he could dig, and—

"Whatcha doing?" a cheerful voice asked.

The Bad Hat glanced up to see Jack panting and wagging his tail. "Um, just thinking," he said.

"'Bout what?" Jack asked curiously.

Escape. Adventures. *Freedom.* "I don't know," the Bad Hat said. "Some private stuff."

"Oh." Jack thought about that. "Okay. Want to play?"

Not really, no. So, the dog shook his head.

But, Jack was running around him in tight circles, barking like crazy, and nipping at his legs.

"Hey!" the dog said. "Knock it off!"

"*Make* me," Jack said.

Okay, he would worry about escaping later. Right now, there were more pressing matters at hand. The dog began to chase him—Jack was a surprisingly shifty and elusive little guy—and they raced around the meadow together. The Bad Hat would, of course, have been lying, if he had said that he didn't like scuffling and wrestling. *A lot.* Especially when he head-butted Jack, who went flying about twenty feet.

Jack scrambled up, like a shaggy little jumping bean. "Think you're tough, because you're a big guy?"

Yes. "Yes," the Bad Hat said.

"Yeah, well, if you're tough, I'm—" Jack paused to think. "I'm the Queen of England."

The Bad Hat shrugged. "Whatever you say, Your Royal Highness."

Instead of being insulted, Jack looked serene. "I think you're embarrassed, because you're way too big and clumsy."

Well, you know, he actually *was* kind of clumsy. People were always yelling at him for knocking things over, but he couldn't help it. He had big feet, and long legs, and he just wasn't very graceful.

A Brindle Pit Bull mix named Josephine came galloping over to them. "I get to go today! I get to go!"

Jack nodded. "I know. That is *wicked* excellent."

Sometimes, the Bad Hat felt as though the rest of the world might be five or six steps ahead of him. He figured he was probably reasonably smart, but he had a lot of— gaps. "Um, where you going?"

"The adoption fair," Josephine said happily. "I can't wait!"

Nope, he was still out of step. "What's an adoption fair?" he asked.

"Oh." Josephine stopped romping after a monarch butterfly for a moment. "Well, it's a fair. And people come to our booth and pat us and take pictures. And then, maybe, they adopt us!"

If he asked, *What's a fair?* or *What's a booth?* they were going to think he was an idiot.

Which he maybe was.

"They have it on the village green," Josephine said. "Or in the gym at the high school, if it's raining. And there's food, and exhibits, and music, and a bunch of people walk by and ask if they can take us home."

What was a village green? Oh, well, the food part sounded interesting, anyway. "Have you ever been to an adoption fair?" he asked Jack.

Jack nodded enthusiastically. "I got to go to the one in July. It was *so fun*. I know all of the people really liked me, but—" Now, he faltered. "Well, I didn't meet anyone who I thought was interesting enough to take me home."

There was an awkward silence.

"Well, sure, that makes sense," the Bad Hat said. "Next time, maybe."

"That's right!" Jack said, back to his normal cocky self. "They'll be *lining up* for the chance to adopt me."

For Jack's sake, the Bad Hat certainly hoped so.

"I bet they will," Josephine said in an encouraging voice. Then, she scampered off to chase the butterfly some more.

"Hey, maybe we'll get adopted together," Jack said.

"And then, we could live in the same house, and be best friends forever!"

The Bad Hat blinked. "We're best friends?" Since when?

"Of course we are," Jack said. "Didn't you know that?"

Nope. And, the thought kind of made him shudder.

Jack tilted his head uncertainly. "You *want* to be my best friend, right?"

Well, except for the part where he was a proud and independent loner, destined to wander the world by himself, causing trouble and searching for fame and adventure and all.

"Right?" Jack asked.

The little Terrier's eyes were so full of hope, that the Bad Hat wasn't sure how to answer. He didn't want to hurt the squirt's feelings. "Sorry, little man, that's not really my thing. I've never had any friends," he said finally. "So, I don't think I know how to do that." Didn't even want to learn how, for that matter.

"Don't worry," Jack said. "I can teach you. I have lots of friends. But, *you're* my favorite!"

To the Bad Hat's surprise, hearing that made him feel kind of warm inside. Almost like a normal, carefree dog. "That's really nice of you," he said. "But, it's not—could we maybe start off by being colleagues?"

Jack stared at him. *"Colleagues?"*

Well, it sounded better than "prison acquaintances." "Sorry," the Bad Hat said. "That's the best I can do."

"You're very strange," Jack said, "but, okay. For now, we'll be *colleagues*."

It was quiet for a moment.

"Are colleagues allowed to head-butt each other?" the dog asked.

Jack laughed. "Yes!"

Well, okay, then. That didn't sound too awful. "All right," the Bad Hat said. "It's a deal."

"Yay!" Jack said, and dashed away across the meadow. "Catch me if you can!"

Piece of cake. The Bad Hat loped after him, closing the distance in a few long strides. Then, he head-butted him across a bed of bright yellow dandelions.

Being colleagues might actually be fun!

CHAPTER FOUR

After lunch, several of the animals, including Josephine, were loaded into a big van full of pet carriers. All of the remaining dogs stood in their outside runs to watch.

"We'll get to go next time, I'm sure of it," Jack said.

Whatever. But, the Bad Hat nodded pleasantly.

"You bet, Jack," MacNulty said, striding back and forth in the concrete run on the other side of the Bad Hat's kennel. He had so much energy that he paced nonstop most of the time during the day, and the rescue group people seemed to be worried that he might have, like, Dog Attention Deficit Disorder. Border Collie Inactivity Disorder, more likely.

"I'm not going to let them put a light blue ribbon on

me next time," Jack said. "I think it made me look a little frou-frou."

The Bad Hat thought that all small dogs, including Terriers, were sort of *innately* frou-frou. "Oh, yeah, don't let them do that to you," he said. "Have some dignity, little man."

"I actually looked cuter than a bug's ear," Jack said, sounding defensive. "I just want to, you know, set a different tone next time. Be sort of outdoorsy and all."

The Bad Hat nodded. "Get a black leather collar with spikes on it. You'll be awesome that way."

Jack looked eager. "I bet I will, yeah. Thanks, Bad Hat!"

"No problem. Here to serve," the Bad Hat said.

Or not.

The afternoon seemed to drag by, although lunch was a definite highlight. Most of the dogs took long naps, and the Bad Hat was quite sure that the cats were all sleeping inside the house. Of course, cats seemed to nap about twenty-two hours a day, so that wasn't anything unusual.

The Bad Hat was really bored. So, he paced for a while, matching his steps with MacNulty's.

"Remember," MacNulty said sternly. "You and I are only *colleagues*, not friends."

Great. The dog sighed. "He told you that?"

"Told *everyone*," MacNulty said.

Super. "Do you like 'compatriots' better?" the dog asked.

MacNulty shook his head.

Okay, whatever. But, he was still going to keep a polite, professional distance from all of them. "Anyway. How come Pico doesn't have a kennel, like the rest of us?" he asked.

"She has arthritis," MacNulty said, jittering around. "So, it wouldn't be comfortable for her. She usually sleeps on Thomas and Joan's bed, I think, or by the fireplace, or on the floor in the office. Cole says they took her off the website, but I'm not sure why."

It was easy enough to figure out *why*. "Because they're keeping her," the Bad Hat said. "Why else?"

"Oh." MacNulty paused, holding a front paw and a back paw in midair. "You know, you might be right about that."

Of course he was right. He was *always* right. Soon, they would figure that out—and worship at his shrine. "They're keeping Florence, too," the Bad Hat said.

57

Jack, who was sprawled out in his kennel in the sun, opened his eyes. "What? No way. Florence is unadoptable. You know, because of her zillions of disabilities and medical conditions."

And the cranky-pants thing. But, he could see the front porch of the house from his kennel, and the truth was pretty obvious. Joan was sitting in a rocking chair, and Florence was on her lap, purring and smacking her with a front paw every so often. Joan would just laugh and keep patting her. The main thing the Bad Hat noticed was that they both looked very pleased with each other.

"The reason Florence is unadoptable is because she *already* has a home," he said.

MacNulty shrugged. "We all do, sort of. Until we get to go to our real homes with our new families."

Nope, not in this case. "Florence *is* home," the Bad Hat said. "Look at them. Joan is her *person*."

Jack tried to peer around him. When that didn't work, he leaped up and down, to try and see past him.

"Why don't you just ask me to move over?" the Bad Hat suggested.

"Oh." Jack stopped jumping. "That sure would be easier."

No kidding. The Bad Hat took a few steps backwards, out of the way.

Jack glanced at the porch. "So, Joan's patting her. What's the big deal? She pats all of us."

"No, really *look* at them," the Bad Hat said. "They're a team. They're pretending she's unadoptable, so that she gets to stay here."

"Oh." Jack watched as Florence swung a shaky paw at Joan, with surprisingly good aim. "How come when people come to visit, I hear them say, 'What's wrong with that cat,' and all?"

The trembling and staggering and everything were all sort of startling, at first, but seemed normal, after a while. "I'm just telling you I see love there, little man," the Bad Hat said. Which made him feel sad, because he couldn't imagine what it would be like to be really *loved* by a person. Not loved, because he was a dog, and the person happened to like dogs and was friendly to him. How would it feel to be loved because someone thought he was truly *special*? Because he was a *specific* dog? Not that it would ever happen—but, still. Thinking about it made him feel wistful.

And that maybe he should stop drinking the water

here, if he was going to go and think adoption thoughts.

"Well, that's good," Jack said. "Because this place would fall apart without Florence. She runs the show."

It certainly seemed that way. And it was good to see that she had a bond with someone who appreciated her. Florence had clearly had a pretty rough time, so it made him feel happy that she was now safe and secure and loved.

If, that is, he was prone to emotion, and cared about stuff like that.

Which everyone knew that he didn't.

At all.

Not even a tiny bit.

The long, lazy afternoon poked along, but everyone woke up instantly and ran outside when the van turned onto the dirt driveway, returning from the adoption fair. An unfamiliar white SUV was trundling right behind it, its tires raising clouds of dust in the air.

"Yo, someone got picked," Lancelot said quietly.

The other dogs nodded, looking very serious.

Why was he always lost? "What do you mean?" the Bad Hat asked.

"Adopters," Lancelot said. "They must have picked someone, and they're coming here to fill out the paper-work and get approved and everything."

"Maybe they'll want two dogs," Jack said. "And they'll take me, too!"

The Bad Hat could feel a surge of hope racing around the kennels, so all of the other dogs must have been wishing the same thing. He wasn't about to upset them by saying that it was very unlikely, and what did he know, anyway? The people *might* want two dogs. But, he would be careful to look distant and unapproachable, so that they wouldn't be tempted to pick *him*. In fact, he decided to lie down on the cement and pretend to be resting.

The van and the four-wheel-drive car had now stopped in the driveway. Some people were getting out of the car, looking excited. A family. Two parents, and a little boy. But, all of *his* former owners had looked excited, too, on that first day. It had worn off pretty fast.

"They're coming, they're coming, they're coming!" Jack shouted.

Talk about destroying a fellow's much-needed sleep. The Bad Hat opened his eyes. "Who's coming?"

"The people!" Jack said. "They'll come out here to

see us now. And maybe they'll adopt a bunch of us!"

The Bad Hat was *so* not interested.

Jack ran to the main door of his kennel. "Come and see, Bad Hat, it's exciting!"

He didn't want to crush the little guy's enthusiasm, so the Bad Hat dragged himself up and went inside.

"Think they're looking for me?" Jack asked. "I hope they're looking for me. I'm right there, on the website. Cole showed me. And I'm *wicked* photogenic."

As far as the Bad Hat knew, he had never been photographed as anything other than a blur of black fur.

Once the family began walking down the corridor, Jack got so charged up that the Bad Hat could hear him jumping wildly and bouncing off the walls.

"Well, that's a cute little dog," a woman's voice remarked. "He has quite a lot to say, doesn't he?"

And how.

"Wow, look at him jump!" a little boy's voice said. "I can't believe how high off the floor he can get!"

"Jack is quite a special dog," Joan said. "He's going to make such a wonderful companion for someone."

The little boy giggled. "He licked my hand. It feels funny."

"That means he likes you," the little boy's mother said. "I can tell you're going to be a really good dog person."

"I am," the boy said proudly. "And I'll help with the walks, and the feeding, and *everything*."

His parents laughed.

"Well, we're planning to hold you to that, Freddy," his father said.

Knowing that the people were going to walk by his kennel next, the Bad Hat went to sit in the far corner, facing away from them.

"That's a beautiful Retriever," the man said. "What's his name?"

"Webster," Joan answered. "He's our newest rescue. We're still getting to know him."

"Hey, Webster," the little boy said. "Come here, boy!"

The Bad Hat stayed where he was, ignoring all of them. If he didn't act friendly, there was no chance anyone would be interested in adopting him.

"He doesn't like me," the little boy said, with his voice quavering.

The Bad Hat sighed. Yes, he was an antisocial grouch, but that didn't mean that he wanted to make small children cry. So, he got up and went over to the door, and allowed the little boy to reach through and pat him on the head.

"He does like me!" the little boy said happily.

The Bad Hat let him pat him for another few seconds, and then went back to sit in the corner.

"That was great," Joan said to the little boy. "That's as friendly and responsive as he's been to anyone so far. Thank you!"

The little boy beamed, and he and his parents continued down the hall, admiring each of the dogs in turn.

All of the dogs were barking and jumping up against their kennel doors to greet the adopters. There was a rumor that the family had filed an application to adopt Josephine and had been approved, and that they were going to have a private meet-and-greet session with her, to make sure it was a good adoption match. But, that didn't stop all of the dogs around the Bad Hat from hoping that the people might decide that they wanted to bring home *two* dogs.

Even he couldn't resist going out to his fenced-in run to watch as the family played with Josephine in the meadow, and got to know her better. Josephine barked, and rolled, and scampered with the little boy, while his parents watched with big smiles on their faces.

"Someone's going home tonight," MacNulty said quietly.

The Bad Hat nodded. It certainly looked that way.

When he had been in other shelters, it had always been difficult for the animals when someone else got adopted. They were all happy for their lucky friend—but, it was hard not to be envious, too.

The first time he had been adopted, he was only about five months old, and still growing—a lot. So, when a young couple came into the pound and wanted to give him a home, he was overjoyed. It was fun, at first, and they seemed to like him when he only weighed about twenty pounds. By the time he hit thirty-five pounds, they were losing interest, and when it was clear he was only half grown, they decided that he was "too big," and gave him away—to a guy who *also* didn't like him, and abandoned him at a local animal shelter late one rainy night, by tying his leash to the locked back door.

That had been a terrifying night, and he'd been really hungry, and so cold that he couldn't stop shaking the whole time.

When the first shelter worker arrived in the morning

to open up for the day, instead of saying something gentle like, *Let's get you dried off, you poor pup,* he groaned and said, "Oh no, not another one."

There was always a lot of talk in the shelters about no one wanting to adopt black dogs. And when a stray dog was old, or sick, or had behavior problems, really bad things that the Bad Hat couldn't even *think* about would usually happen.

He was in that particular shelter for a couple of weeks, crammed into a small cage with a cold concrete floor. Then, he was put in a truck, with about fifty other dogs, and they drove for about two days, until he ended up somewhere in New Hampshire—at yet another shelter. That was where the mean family had come and picked him out—before getting rid of him.

So, yeah, he had earned the right to be cynical and grumpy. But, that didn't mean that watching Josephine dance happily around in the meadow with the boy and his parents wasn't breaking his heart a little.

After a while, Josephine and the family went into the house, and were inside for what seemed like hours.

"Finishing the paperwork," MacNulty said.

Seemed likely, yeah. The Bad Hat nodded.

Finally, the family came outside again, with the little

boy proudly walking Josephine on a brand-new blue leash. The parents shook hands with Joan and Thomas, who both leaned down to give Josephine a farewell hug.

Josephine wagged her tail so hard that her whole body shook.

"Bye!" she barked towards the kennels, right before she got into the car. "I'll miss you guys!"

They all barked things back like, "Good luck!" and "We'll miss you, too!" and "Have fun!"

After the SUV drove down the driveway and out of sight, it got very quiet in the kennels. Jack turned and went inside, without saying anything. The Bad Hat heard him lie down on his bed and start crying. Crying *hard.*

To his shock, the Bad Hat almost started crying, too.

"Hey, come on, cheer up, little man," he said. "Everything's okay. One of these days, it's going to be your turn, too."

Jack kept crying.

"You're really cute," the Bad Hat said. "People won't be able to resist you. Seriously."

Jack wept even harder. "They've been resisting me for *months.* No one is *ever* going to love me."

It was hard to disagree with that, when the Bad Hat felt the exact same way. But, then again, Jack was actually friendly and eager to be chosen by someone—which would have to help him be able to find a new home.

The sadness must have been contagious, because within a minute or two, almost every single dog in the kennels was crying. *Sobbing*, even.

In fact, the truth was, the Bad Hat curled up on his bed in a tight ball, and cried, too.

A little.

Maybe.

CHAPTER FIVE

T he Bad Hat wasn't sorry that he, personally, hadn't gotten adopted—even though the little boy and his parents had seemed nice and fun and genuine. But, because all of the other dogs wanted so much to find homes, and people who would love them—and maybe none of them would *ever* get adopted, which was really, really awful—he cried. And cried. And then, cried some more.

After listening to nonstop weeping throughout the kennels for what felt like a really long time, he finally heard a tiny stump, stump, skitter, skitter coming down the hall.

"It's okay, everyone," Florence said, in soothing meows. "Josephine is going to be very happy, and you all will find homes someday, too. Joan and Thomas will make *sure* of that. So, please don't be upset."

No one stopped crying.

"And there are some positively brilliant liver-flavored biscuits baking in the kitchen," Florence said. "I'm sure Monica will bring them in here for all of you, while they're still warm, and they will taste *delicious*. And then, everyone can go out to the meadow, and run and run until the sun goes down."

The dogs kept crying. Whimpering. Wailing. Sobbing. Wrenching, terrible, heart-breaking sobs.

The Bad Hat heard Florence sigh. Then, she stumped over to his door—and looked stunned.

"Are you crying, too, Bad Hat?" she asked.

Caught in the act. "Nope," the Bad Hat said, and was embarrassed that his bark cracked and sounded squeaky. He quickly got up, shook himself all over, and tried not to sniffle audibly as he strode to the door. "I'm too cool to cry."

"Maybe you have allergies," Florence said kindly.

That was it. Allergies! The Bad Hat nodded. "Yeah, it's the pollen, that's all. Or—leaves. Autumn leaves bother me. Are the cats crying, too?"

"Most of them, yes," Florence said.

Wow. "Does this happen every time someone gets adopted?" the Bad Hat asked.

Florence sighed again. "I'm afraid so. It's worse for the ones who have been here for a long time, although some of them, like Cole, have given up on ever finding a home. So, they just shrug it off, and pretend they don't care, and in some ways, that's even *more* sad."

He had never thought of it that way, but maybe it was true. It was hard to decide what was worse—having hopes that never came true, or having no hopes at all. "Do you think those people will be good to Josephine?" he asked.

Florence nodded. "Indubitably. Their application and references were very carefully checked, and there will be home visits to make sure. Also, the adopters have to promise that if, for any reason, it isn't working out, they will bring the animal back here. No one will *ever* end up in a public shelter again."

The Bad Hat didn't believe that, but he was sure that Joan and Thomas meant well, and always tried as hard as they could to make things work out.

"Who is the most upset?" Florence asked.

71

The Bad Hat motioned with his head in the direction of Jack's cage.

"Okay, thank you," Florence said, and limped over to the kennel next door, where Jack was still sobbing miserably. "Jack," she said. "You are adorable and charming. You *will* be adopted. I promise."

"I was jumping really high, and doing spins in the air, and they didn't even *care*," Jack said, through his tears.

"Of course they cared," Florence said. "But, their application for Josephine had already been approved, so she was going home with them."

Jack kept crying.

"When you *do* get adopted, Jack, I'll be the one sitting here weeping," Florence said. "Because you are my dear friend, and I shall miss you terribly. But, I'll be glad, too, because you will be going off to a wonderful new life."

Jack sniffled so hard that he sneezed. "I'll miss you, too, Florence. And be really sad that you're unadoptable."

Not that he was eavesdropping or anything, but the Bad Hat laughed.

"Right, I forgot," Jack said. "The Bad Hat says that Joan is, like, your person, and that you are *already* adopted."

Florence laughed, too. "The Bad Hat may have a little bit of cat in him."

Oh, gross. No way. "I am *all* dog," the Bad Hat said. "In fact, I'm a dog and a half! All other dogs bow before me."

Duke—who had been crying in his kennel across the corridor—perked up. "They actually *bow*? How'd you manage that? Florence, you're not going to rename him King, are you? Because I'm still trying to work my way back up."

"No, he's the Bad Hat," Florence said. "It rather suits him."

Raw-ther. The British accent cracked him up, so the Bad Hat laughed again.

"Don't worry, Duke," Florence said, ignoring that. "You may still try to earn your promotion."

"Whew," Duke said, and flopped back down on his bed.

The connecting door to the house opened, and the smell of baked liver and cheese and other good things came wafting into the hall.

"Oh my, so much howling and yowling back here," Monica said, in her friendly way. "What a ruckus you dear little things are making. But, you're all going to have some nice biscuits now, and cheer up."

At least six of the dogs yelled, "Biscuits! Biscuits! Biscuits!"—and now, everyone was barking instead of crying.

Since he was so very resistant to congeniality and the Ways of the Civilized World, the Bad Hat stubbornly decided not to eat his fresh dog biscuits right away. In fact, he lasted almost two full minutes before devouring them.

Then, a couple of volunteers whose names he didn't know came in and took turns leading everyone outside to the meadow. The dogs mostly forgot how unhappy they had been, and romped energetically. Except for a little bit of goofing around with Jack, the Bad Hat was determined to keep to himself. But, when Rachel, a grey-and-white Greyhound mix, challenged him to a race, he took her up on it.

She was *fast*. The Bad Hat realized that he wasn't going to be able to keep pace, so he gave her back hip a quick bump with his shoulder. It knocked her off balance, and she slowed down enough to stare at him.

"What do you think you're doing?" she asked.

Wasn't it obvious? The Bad Hat shrugged. "I hate to lose."

Rachel looked puzzled. "But, that's cheating."

Was it? Not really. "No, it's *gamesmanship*," the Bad Hat said. "It's not the same at all."

Rachel narrowed her eyes. "What's the difference?"

It was a jock thing, and someone either got it, or not. She seemed to fall right smack into the *not* category. "I wanted to win, but you were faster, so I knocked you down," the Bad Hat said.

Rachel frowned. "Just like that?"

Yep.

Lancelot, who was jumping around with a skinny little Spaniel mix named Matilda, laughed. "Dude, that is so totally twisted. You're going to be a really good villain."

Oh, yeah. He was going to be a *fabulous* villain. And a ne'er-do-well, and a punk, and all of that other great stuff.

The rest of the dogs kept playing, but after a while, the Bad Hat wandered over to the fence by himself. He stood there, gauging the height. It looked pretty high, but it really wasn't. He would need a running start, but if he put a good effort into it, he could almost certainly jump high enough to be able to scramble over the top and escape.

Which was, of course, his goal, but did he want to do

it *today*? Right after everyone had finally stopped crying? Maybe he should bide his time.

Not that they would all go to pieces, if he left—but, still. This wasn't the right moment.

Jack bounced over next to him. "What's up, buddy?"

Buddy? Okay, *definitely* not today. He didn't want to have Jack dissolve into tears twice in less than an hour. "Just thinking," he said.

Jack shrugged. "Okay. You sure do that a lot, Bad Hat. But, want to chase our tails, instead? That would be *so fun.*"

There were worse ways to spend an hour, yeah. "I'll watch you, little man," the Bad Hat said. "Then, maybe I'll join in."

"Okay!" Jack said. He chased his tail in one direction, stopped to scratch for a few seconds, and then chased his tail wildly in the other direction.

"That's a pretty dumb game," the Bad Hat said.

Jack reversed direction, and chased his tail some more. "That's probably why it's fun."

Well, yeah. Dog games had never been famous for their complexity. The Bad Hat liked to think of himself as being unusually intelligent and clever—but, that didn't make it true.

"Can I climb on your back and look around?" Jack asked. "See what it's like to be big?"

What? No! "Of course you can't," the Bad Hat said.

"Come on, colleague, bend your legs a little, so I can climb up," Jack said impatiently.

He was never going to live down the colleague crack, was he? The Bad Hat sighed, and lowered his front paws and shoulders. "Fine. But, just for a minute."

"Yay!" Jack said, and scrabbled his way up.

The Bad Hat winced. "Ow. You need to have your claws clipped."

"I know," Jack said, very cheerful. "I was really bad the last time they tried, so they postponed it."

Great. The dog stood patiently, resisting the urge to shake Jack off.

Jack looked around, balancing precariously, digging those annoying claws in. "Wow, it must be cool to be this tall."

Yeah. Although the Bad Hat was pretty sure he would be cool no matter *how* big he was.

Jack enjoyed the view for a while longer, and then jumped down to the grass. "Want to chase our tails some more?"

Why not. "Sure," the Bad Hat said—and that was what they did, until it was time to go inside again.

After midnight, all of the animals gathered in the den for snacks and movies. They watched *E.T.*—which made most of them cry again, during the sad scenes. But, it was still a really good movie, and the dog was glad they had chosen it. Next, they watched a movie called *The Blind Side*—which was about football, and so, in the Bad Hat's opinion, a fine viewing choice.

They were going to watch a third movie, but it was close to dawn, and it would take a while for everyone to get back to their kennels without being seen. So, they made sure that the television was off, the kibble bags were dragged out of sight, and the room looked neat and orderly, as though none of them had ever been in there.

"I liked the movies," Jack said drowsily from his bed.

Hard to disagree with that. The snacks had been good, too. "Yep," the Bad Hat said, and decided that he sounded just like a cowboy. All terse, and laconic, and heroically aloof.

"Do you really think Josephine will be happy?" Jack asked.

"Yup," the Bad Hat said. Did he want to be a cowboy, instead of a villain? Maybe, yeah. Although it was so hard to *choose*.

"That's good," Jack said, and yawned. "Someday, we will be, too. See you tomorrow, best friend. I mean, colleague!"

In spite of his better instincts, that made the Bad Hat smile. "You bet, little man," he said.

It was colder the next day, but they were still all eager to run in the meadow for most of the morning. Then, it was time for lunch, and long naps. Thomas came to get the Bad Hat at one point, and brought him to the examination room, for a quick checkup by Dr. K., who reported that his ribs were healing beautifully. The Bad Hat didn't go out of his way to be friendly, but he cooperated with the exam and stood without moving the entire time. He was very glad, though, when it was time to go back to his kennel for another nap.

After supper was over—they had hamburger and yoghurt with their kibble!—the dogs were restless, because everyone could feel a storm coming. It was going to be something called a nor'easter, which the Bad Hat thought was a mighty fancy Yankee way to describe a little wind and rain. He wasn't sure what the big deal was, but the rest of the animals were edgy, and for once, MacNulty wasn't the only one pacing around.

So far, there was just a cool breeze in the air, and it was drizzling a little, and the Bad Hat had no trouble nodding off.

But, around ten o'clock, the rain really started coming down and the wind intensified. It was a serious downpour now, and the pressure from the wind made the Bad Hat's ears hurt. They all stayed inside the warm, enclosed parts of their kennels, and away from the outdoor runs. The storm was a lot more powerful than the Bad Hat had expected, and he was glad to be indoors.

To make matters worse, right before midnight, the power went out, and it was suddenly completely dark.

"Oh, no," MacNulty groaned. "No movies or TV tonight."

That was disappointing, but then again, the Bad Hat felt snug and sleepy on his soft bed. So, it might be okay to have a full night's rest for once. One thing he had learned during the past couple of days was that afternoon naps just didn't make up for gallivanting and hobnobbing all night, every night.

After a while, Thomas and Joan came through the corridor, holding flashlights and battery-powered lanterns. They checked every kennel to make sure that all of the dogs were okay, and stopped to comfort some of the more anxious ones. Matilda was shivering uncontrollably, and by craning his neck, the Bad Hat saw Joan strap her into some kind of little jacket. Once she was wearing it, Matilda wagged her tail and settled down onto her bed.

"That's a ThunderShirt," Jack said. "Makes bad weather seem less scary."

Which made no sense. "How does it do that?" the Bad Hat asked.

"I don't know," Jack said. "One time, during a thunderstorm, I pretended I was all upset, so I could try one on."

That figured. "Did you like it?" the Bad Hat asked.

Jack thought about that. "Well, it was snug, so that was sort of nice. But then, it got wicked hot, and I had to pitch a fit so they would take it off me."

These New England animals loved using the word "wicked" to describe things. It was peculiar. But, the image of Jack kicking and writhing and making a scene—in a too-tight jacket—was pretty funny.

After a while, even the really nervous dogs relaxed,

and the Bad Hat fell asleep to the sound of pounding rain and howling winds. Thomas and Joan had left two of the battery-powered storm lanterns in the hall, so it wasn't as dark and spooky anymore.

He wasn't sure what time it was when a violent crashing sound woke him up. Then, something heavy smashed into his kennel so hard that it felt like the whole building shook.

He leaped to his feet, barking out a fierce "Whoa!"

All around him, the other dogs had also woken up. Everyone was asking what happened, and if anyone was hurt.

"I think a branch fell," Lancelot said. "There's leaves and stuff in my run."

"There's leaves and stuff in my *water dish*," Jack said. "Yuck! How am I going to drink it, when it's all gross like that?"

"I think it's a tree," MacNulty said. "It looks like there's a tree on top of my kennel."

The Bad Hat peeked out through his swinging door, not sure what to expect. But, it was definitely a fallen tree, and it had pretty much crushed his section of chain link fence. There were so many branches and leaves that he couldn't see into the exercise runs on either side.

"You okay, little man?" he asked. "You okay, MacNulty?"

They both yelled, "Yes!"—which was a relief.

"Looks like you got the worst of it, Bad Hat," MacNulty said. "Mine isn't so messed up."

"Mine's okay, too," Jack said. "Except for my water, which is, like, *ruined.* I hope I can wait until morning, for them to clean it out." He coughed experimentally. "But, I don't know. I'm suddenly wicked thirsty."

Such a baby. Weren't Terriers supposed to be tough? "My fence is broken," the Bad Hat said.

"Wow," one of the dogs from across the hall said. "You're lucky it only fell outside. Your whole cage could have been smashed, and you, along with it!"

What a comforting thought. The Bad Hat wormed his way through some of the thick, wet branches and saw that the end of his kennel had been torn off completely from the force of the tree landing on top of it. So, the kennel was now open.

Open.

Inviting him.

Beckoning.

"The fence isn't attached anymore," he said slowly.

"That's okay," MacNulty said. "They'll fix it in the morning."

With the fence gone, the wind—and the meadow—
smelled even more fresh and tantalizing than usual.

"I could get out," the Bad Hat said.

In fact, he could get out *easily*. Be free, and independent. He ventured forward a few steps, careful not to let
his paws touch any of the sharp metal ends sticking up
from the torn chain-link fencing.

"Don't do it, man," MacNulty said, in a low warning voice.

"Come on, it's right there in front of me," the Bad
Hat said. "Like a *sign*. And I'm an adventurer."

"Fine, whatever," MacNulty said. "But, don't be an
idiot, too."

Was he really supposed to resist such a perfect opportunity? The Bad Hat shook his head and climbed over a
pile of wet branches.

"What's he doing?" Jack asked nervously. "I can't see
anything through the leaves! What are you doing, Bad
Hat?"

"He's going to try to run away," MacNulty said.

No, he wasn't going to try; he was going to *do* it.

"What?!" Jack sounded horrified. "You can't do that,
Bad Hat—you're my best friend!"

"This might be my only chance, little man," the Bad
Hat said. "If I stay here, I'll never know what it's like out

there. And, even worse, I might get adopted again. So, I have to go, while I can."

"But, we might get adopted *together,*" Jack said. "And then, we could always be friends."

Even if he wanted to be adopted, no one who liked a cute, feisty little Terrier would also want a big, clumsy black dog with an attitude problem.

"It's nice of you to say that, but I honestly don't think anyone is ever going to choose me," the Bad Hat said. "Don't worry, I'll be okay out there. And I'll really miss you guys."

As the word quickly spread, more and more dogs were yelling for him to stay, and not to do anything stupid.

What, like "Stupid" wasn't his middle name? "Sorry, guys, a dog's gotta do what a dog's gotta do," the Bad Hat said.

Everyone was yelling, "No!" or "Stop!" except for Jack, who was yelling, "Don't leave me!" All of which made the Bad Hat feel a little guilty.

Okay, he felt *a lot* guilty. Still, he needed to go find his destiny, and maybe even his purpose in the world. And he couldn't do that here, although it was a fairly pleasant place to be, and he *would* miss everyone.

But, still. This was his chance. And he was a dog, looking

at an open door. They were dogs, too. What did they *expect* him to do? Just ignore it? So, he squirmed through a few more branches, and found himself standing outside, on the wet grass.

"Don't," Jack said tearfully. "Please don't."

"I'm sorry, Jack, I just have to go," the Bad Hat said. "But, I'll never forget you. Say good-bye to Florence and the other cats for me. And thanks for being so nice, while I was staying here."

Then, he turned and ran across the grass, heading for the woods. Everyone was shouting for him to come back, but he ignored the barking and ran faster.

It felt good to run. He felt strong. He felt fierce.

He was free!

CHAPTER SIX

The Bad Hat galloped through the woods, splashed across a stream, and raced up the mossy bank on the other side.

Free! Free! Free!

It was excellent. Fabulous, even.

But, wow, he was pretty wet. And it was windy. And other than the fact that this was a place called New Hampshire, he had no idea where he was.

And now, a lot of branches were snapping in the heavy winds and falling all around him. One even bounced off his shoulder! Maybe it would be smart to find some shelter, until the storm was over.

He was a country boy, so the forest didn't scare him.

Even though it was dark.

Really dark.

It was lucky that he was a brave and fearsome fellow, or he might have been tempted to run back to his kennel and pretend that his bold escape attempt had never happened.

There were other animals out here in the forest, but he didn't smell anything ominous. Squirrels, chipmunks, rabbits, deer, skunks, and—well, wait. Skunks weren't his favorite. He would have to be careful to avoid them.

After exploring for a while, he came across a little rock den, which seemed pretty dry. It looked like an ideal place to spend the rest of the night, but he could smell that something was already inside.

Raccoons. Several of them.

"Excuse me," he said politely, from outside the den. "Is there any room in there?"

A pudgy raccoon lumbered over to the entrance, and looked him over.

"Nope, can't help you," the raccoon said. "We don't like dogs, and you're huge, and you're very wet."

"Well, that's the point," the Bad Hat said. "I'm trying to get in from out of the rain."

The raccoon shook his head firmly. "Nope. Sorry. If we

knew you, maybe, but you're a stranger, and domesticated. You would be a corrupting influence on the children."

"I'm abandoning humanity forever," the Bad Hat said. "So, you don't have to worry about me saying anything nice about human beings. I'm totally behind the whole life-in-the-wilderness self-reliance thing."

The raccoon studied him some more, but then shook his head again. "Sorry, large dog. We're pretty cramped in here as it is. But, good luck to you. Please go now, because you're disturbing our rest."

"I thought you guys were nocturnal," the Bad Hat said.

The stocky raccoon shrugged. "Usually we are, but the little ones get tired. And we tend to hunker down in bad weather."

A much smaller raccoon peeked out. "Help! A dog! Don't try to eat us!"

"Don't worry, wee one," the older raccoon said. "I'm just going to give him directions to a pile of logs where he can find some shelter. Go back and lie down."

The young raccoon shrugged. "Okay. Bye, scary dog!"

"Good night," the Bad Hat said. "Sleep well." He shivered a little. "Stay dry!"

The older raccoon gave him a long look, and the Bad Hat tried to look as wet and pathetic and nonthreatening as possible.

"Just for the night?" the dog said, making his voice sound much higher and weaker than normal.

The raccoon sighed. "Okay," he said, and used a long-clawed front paw to draw a distinct line in the dirt. "You can stay until morning, as long as you don't come inside any further than this. And if you snore, all bets are off."

Fair enough. "Thank you," the Bad Hat said. "I'm much obliged."

It was a tight squeeze, but the dog managed to curl up in the dirt, protected from the rain and wind. Freedom was *very* tiring. So, he had no trouble dozing off, even though the raccoons were sleeping with what sounded like a concert of wheezy, little snorts. In fact, he went into such a heavy sleep, that he didn't have any dreams at all, even the normal ones where he was running, and his legs would thrash around.

When he woke up in the morning, the first thing he saw was a pair of yellow beady eyes a couple of inches from his face.

"Yikes!" the Bad Hat yelped. He jumped away from the eyes, bumping his head on the top of the musty den.

"Good morning," a tiny raccoon said. "I wanted to look at you up close."

That was for sure. It would be hard to get *closer* than the little animal had been to his face, without actually climbing on him. The dog quickly went outside the den and stood in the clearing. It was nice to be out in the fresh air again! And even though the ground was muddy and some branches had fallen down, it looked like it was going to be a bright, sunny day.

"I never saw an actual dog before," the baby raccoon explained, following right behind him. "Just pictures in a book we found in the trash once, and my grandpoppy sometimes tells scary stories about you, and what you're all like."

Okay, he now felt compelled to defend his entire species. "Most of us are really very friendly," the Bad Hat said. "No matter what you've heard."

"I don't know." The baby raccoon moved even closer than he had been before, staring with those huge yellow unblinking eyes. "You have funny short fur, and that would make it hard to trust you."

91

"Leave him alone," an adult raccoon—almost certainly the baby's mother—said crossly. "You are being very rude, Morton."

"But, look at his fur!" the little raccoon said, and tapped the Bad Hat's muzzle with his paw. "He feels like an otter! Only, he is way too tall."

"I'm a Retriever," the Bad Hat said. Supposedly, anyway.

"Can you swim?" the little raccoon asked. "All fast and sleek like otters do?"

He had never seen an otter in real life, so it was hard to be sure. "Of course," the Bad Hat said. "Retrievers are *all about* swimming."

"That's awesome," the little raccoon said happily, and then pointed at the rabies tag on his collar. "I like that— it's so shiny! Would you give it to me?"

Why not? "Sure," the Bad Hat said. "But, it's metal, and I don't know how to take it off."

"I bet I can do it," the little raccoon said proudly. "I have opposable thumbs."

Okay, whatever. "Knock yourself out," the Bad Hat said. "If you can pry it off, it's yours."

The little raccoon stood on his hind legs, and twisted and pulled and tugged at the bright red tag. It wasn't exactly comfortable, but the Bad Hat waited patiently for him to finish. Finally, though, the raccoon stopped, out of breath.

"That's really hard," he panted. "Maybe my thumbs aren't opposable *enough*."

The raccoon's brothers and sisters came tumbling out of the den to try and help. When that didn't work, the parents and the grumpy grandfather raccoon also pried at the stubborn metal fastener, without success.

This time yesterday, the Bad Hat had not expected to start off his day standing in the middle of the forest, surrounded by a family of vocal and frustrated raccoons.

"Tell you what," he said, since he was pretty tired of having his neck poked and prodded. "It was very hospitable of you to let me spend the night. Why don't you take the whole collar, and then you can play with *all* of the license tags?"

The young raccoons jumped up and down with excitement, shouting in their squeaky little voices.

"All right, but just this once," their mother said. "And please thank the nice oversized dog for the present."

The little raccoons tugged on his collar until they were able to pull it over his head.

"Thanks, Mr. Huge Dog!" they all said. "You're *nifty*. We like you!"

"You're welcome," the Bad Hat said, just as politely.

He watched for a few minutes while the young raccoons formed a small circle and began throwing the collar back and forth, playing catch with it. They laughed and cheered and erupted into tiny giggles as the tags jingled together in the air.

Well, whatever floated their little boats, right?

The dog felt sort of—naked—without a collar, but, maybe that was a good thing. Now, he was truly a Creature of the Wild. Technically, yes, he had a microchip, which Dr. K. had put in, but it didn't show, and he certainly would not mention it to anyone.

As he trotted away, the baby raccoons yelled, "Thank you!" and then went back to their dancing and giggling.

He wandered through the woods for a while, not sure where he was going or what he was going to do next. There were so many possibilities! Not that he could think of anything specific right now—but, well, he knew the possibilities *existed*.

He noticed that his stomach was growling, and that he was very hungry. That was a serious problem, since he didn't have a bowl! And so, no one was going to come along and put food in it.

The concept of that was so horrifying that he had to sink down into a pile of wet pine needles to absorb it.

No dish. No breakfast. No homemade biscuits.

Wow. This was a serious flaw in his plan to be a rebellious loner.

Should he become a big, bad hunter? Stalk through the wilderness, attacking helpless prey, and surviving by his own wits and skills?

Except, what if the prey turned out to be cute little animals, who snickered and frolicked and were much too adorable to pounce on? That would be awful.

Okay, he would simply forage in trash cans for scraps. It wasn't dignified—but, it would be delicious. To make the plan work, though, he would have to find some houses, first. So far, this part of New Hampshire seemed to be pretty deserted.

He wasn't completely sure where New Hampshire even *was*, except that he knew that it was up north, and that the people—and animals—had funny accents. So, he decided to explore. He walked through the woods for what seemed like a really long time, until he found a road. It was much easier to make his way on pavement, so he trotted along, jumping into the bushes to hide whenever he heard a car coming. Mostly, because he was afraid of cars, but also so that he wouldn't be captured, if anyone came out looking for him.

At first, all he passed were woods and farms, surrounded by green mountains in the distance. The air smelled clean and fresh, and he stopped to breathe deeply every so often.

It was good to be free!

There were horses and cows and sheep and goats and chickens, and sometimes people, and even dogs, on the farms. Some of the farms had big fields, or orchards, and he saw lots of pickup trucks and barns and tractors and plowing equipment. Luckily, no one seemed to notice— or care—that a big black dog was running down the road, with no collar.

There had been so much rain the night before that there were puddles everywhere. So, he could stop and get a long, refreshing drink whenever he wanted. It wasn't as good as a normal breakfast, but it was better than nothing.

After a while, he started passing small houses and cottages. He sniffed experimentally, in case there were any tasty trash cans nearby. But, most of the houses seemed to be empty. No cars, no sign of movement, no indication of anyone living in them.

That was creepy. What if some kind of aliens, or witches, had come and taken all of the people away? Or, what if the people were still here, but they were zombies? He was pretty sure he would have a hard time winning a fight against a bunch of zombies. Besides, if he bit a zombie, he might turn *into* one. That would be terrible.

The Bad Hat slowed his pace, moving more cautiously. Maybe, if he saw anything suspicious, his best plan would be to run away as fast as he could. He was on a dirt road now, and the woods on either side were dark and thick with trees.

Did zombies have a scent? If not, he would be in trouble, because they could jump out at him when he least expected it.

Just in case, he broke into a gallop right away. He was almost certainly faster than the average zombie, right? But, it wouldn't hurt to get a head start.

Should he give up and run home to the rescue group? Although he was pretty far away now, and he had been wandering around so much that it might take him a long time to find it again. Besides, he wanted to have adventures—as long as they were nice adventures. *Safe* adventures.

The woods were seriously thick. Fir trees, and bushes, and all kinds of undergrowth, which made everything seem very dark and mysterious. In addition to zombies, what if there were other scary things? Like lions? And tigers? And maybe even *bears*?

Okay, maybe it was time to turn around and go the other way. It might be safer to—just then, something lunged out of the bushes at him, yelling, "Hey!"

The Bad Hat was so scared, that he heard himself make a sort of squeal, and he sprang straight up into the air to avoid his attacker.

"Wow, that was some *serious* elevation!" his vicious enemy said. "I'm going to give you a nine-point-three for that jump, Bad Hat."

Jack. It was Jack.

The Bad Hat let out his breath, and tried to get his heart to stop beating so hard. "What are you doing here?"

Jack was frowning at his front paw as he examined some mud caked on it. "This is gross. So much nature. Anyway, Florence said it was okay for you to have some adventures, as long as you used the buddy system." Then, he grinned. "Oops, I meant, the *colleague* system."

Well, what kind of dumb idea was *that?* "That doesn't work at all," the Bad Hat said. "I'm a loner. I'm not looking for, you know, a *sidekick.*"

Jack shrugged. "Florence made a rule. I'm just doing what she told me. I would have been here sooner, but I wanted to play in the meadow for a while, and have some breakfast, first."

He'd had *breakfast?* The Bad Hat looked at him enviously. "What did you have?"

Jack thought for a minute. "Well, first, they gave me some nice fresh water in my bowl. And then, kibble, of course. And there was some really good beefy gravy. I had to lick my dish for *a long time* to make sure I got all of it."

Gravy? He'd missed *gravy?* Life was *so* not fair.

"What did you have for breakfast?" Jack asked.

"Muddy water," the Bad Hat said grimly.

"Yuck." Jack made a face. "Glad that was you, not me."

Beef gravy. Oh, the *humanity.* The Bad Hat sighed. "Are Joan and Thomas searching for me and all?"

Jack nodded. "Thomas is driving around in the van,

I think. I was maybe going to try and get a ride with him, to save time, but Florence said that wouldn't be very savvy. So, I walked about a million miles to come find you, instead."

This was a whole lot of unfortunate information all at once, and the Bad Hat sat down in the middle of the road to think.

"So, what happens now?" Jack asked.

Good question. "Well, my whole plan is *ruined*, if I'm not on my own," the Bad Hat said.

"Is it making you even grumpier than usual?" Jack asked.

Yes. "You can go home, and tell Florence I'm just fine," the Bad Hat said. "Because you've totally interrupted my schedule, and I want to go back to exploring."

"I'll go with you," Jack said.

The Bad Hat shook his head. "Nope. No way. I need my privacy."

Jack shrugged. "Okay, I'll walk ten feet in front of you. That way, I'm doing what I'm supposed to do, but you can have some personal space."

"In front of me?" the Bad Hat said. "What, are you kidding? Behind me, *maybe*, but even that's not a good situation. I want to be alone, don't you get that?"

Jack gave him an injured look. "You are so weird, Bad Hat. I'm just, like, following protocol, you know? And you're hurting my feelings."

The Bad Hat frowned.

"*A lot,*" Jack said. "You were supposed to be happy to see me, not all cranky and mean."

Had Jack not *met* him before? "I'm always cranky and mean," the Bad Hat said.

"Yeah, but you abandoned me last night, and ran away, and now, even though I gave up my nap to come and keep you company, you're not being *welcoming.*" Jack sniffled a little. "It's not right." He sniffled again. "It's not *nice.*"

Nowhere—not even on a single page—in the Bad Hat Handbook, did it say that he was ever required to be nice.

Jack brushed his muddy paw across his eyes. "I am so sad right now."

Was he going to pull out a violin next? "Okay, okay," the Bad Hat said impatiently. "How about if I let you walk with me for one hour?"

"That's all?" Jack asked.

"It's very generous," the Bad Hat said.

"Not hardly, but okay." Jack took one step forward, then stopped. "We don't have watches, and I don't see any clocks. How will we know how much time has passed?"

So much nitpicking. It was exhausting. "We'll estimate," the Bad Hat said.

Jack looked dubious. "That's not very scientific."

"Then, we'll figure it out from the position of the sun in the sky," the Bad Hat said.

Jack cocked his head. "Seriously?"

Yes. The Bad Hat decided that he was tired of worrying about details, so he just started walking down the road.

"Wait up!" Jack said, and trotted after him.

The dog set a fairly brisk pace. He had things to do and places to see, even if he wasn't sure what any of them were.

"If we can't have an effortless conversation while we run, we're going too fast," Jack panted.

"Can't we run quietly and commune with nature?" the Bad Hat asked.

"No," Jack said. "We're supposed to talk about our lives, and *bond*." Then, he laughed. "Look at your expression! Man, are you easy to scare! It's okay, we can just walk around."

Whew. They didn't have to bond. Relaxing a little, the Bad Hat slowed down, so that Jack would have an easier time keeping up.

There were small houses tucked in among the trees, and they could see long, steep, winding driveways. The Bad Hat was also relieved to notice some signs of life here and there. Shades up, lights on, cars in the driveways, and he caught the scents of people, and even some pets, inside a few of the cottages. Once, he even smelled breakfast cooking—bacon and eggs and toast—and the smell was so enticing that he stopped in his tracks to sniff it for as long as possible.

Wow, was he hungry. "Do you smell that?" he asked. "Bacon and everything!"

"Bet you're sorry you missed out on the gravy," Jack said.

He was extremely sorry.

As they rounded a curve, the Bad Hat saw the shimmer of water, and realized that a lot of the houses were near a big, beautiful lake. In fact, there were a bunch of cottages built right along the shoreline. They made their way through the woods and down to the water's edge, so that they could get a closer look.

There were rustic cabins, pretty cottages, tiny grassy

lawns, pine and birch trees, wooden docks, and lots of small boats pulled up onto the land or anchored to little buoys. Canoes, rowboats, kayaks, sailboats, and a few motorboats. A range of forest-green mountains rose up above the lake, and he could see a bunch of other cottages over there on the other side.

"This is nice," Jack said.

The Bad Hat had to agree. If this was what New Hampshire was like, it was a pretty cool place.

They stood there, and admired the view for a while.

It was such a beautiful lake! And the air smelled so pure! When the Bad Hat had been back in Arkansas, he had gone swimming in a pond once, and it had been really fun, even though he saw a water moccasin and had to dash back to shore, as fast as his puppy legs would take him. A lake this large and beautiful would be even *more* fun to swim in. Especially if there weren't any snakes. Or eels, or snapping turtles, or—well, at least the lake *looked* pretty.

"Let's go check it out," he said, and trotted down one of the driveways, which sloped down to the edge of the water.

"Okay, but don't get too close," Jack said. "We don't want to get wet."

Terriers were wimps. *Of course*, they wanted to get wet!

It was windy, and the Bad Hat closed his eyes, so that he could focus on all of the interesting smells in the air. The water was lapping softly against the rocky shore, and it was a soothing sound. Maybe they should take a swim, and then find a comfortable spot where they could settle down, and enjoy a nap in the sunshine?

"We should go swimming," he said.

Jack shook his head. "No way. It looks too cold."

The Bad Hat stuck his front paw in the water to test the temperature. A little chilly, but not enough to make him yelp.

"Is it awful?" Jack asked, quivering slightly at the very thought.

"No, it feels good," the Bad Hat said, and checked the water with his paw again. Hmmm. Maybe not *chilly*, so much as *icy*.

Rough and tough as he was, perhaps he should wait until the sun was higher in the sky, and warmed the water up a little? It wasn't as though they were on a tight schedule.

"It looks deep, too," Jack said uneasily.

Certainly, the Bad Hat would go ahead and swim right now, if he really felt like it. He just didn't, that's all. It had absolutely nothing to do with the temperature.

"Well, if you're going to be a big baby about the water,

we can go explore someplace else," the Bad Hat said magnanimously.

"Fine with me," Jack said, already heading up the driveway.

They were loping back up to the dirt road, when they heard a strange sound and stopped to look at each other.

"What was that?" Jack asked.

The Bad Hat listened more carefully. *Glurg?* Or *glurp?* Weird. Like a person was trying to talk, with a mouthful of water. Which seemed like a dumb idea to him, but who was he to judge?

Except now the sound suddenly seemed panicky. It was coming from out in the lake somewhere, but the Bad Hat couldn't see anything other than the various boats, some small, choppy waves, and a few big rocks. Nothing particularly alarming.

The mysterious noise echoed weakly across the water again, and this time, it sounded like a waterlogged "Help!"

Someone was in trouble out there!

CHAPTER SEVEN

He and Jack stared at each other.

"What do we do?" Jack asked.

"I don't know," the Bad Hat said, and squinted out at the lake. It was hard to see if there might be a person's head out there, bobbing in the strong current.

"Help!" the voice yelled, and now he saw an arm wave frantically in the water, a couple hundred yards away.

Even though he had renounced all contact with human beings for the rest of his life, and was seriously considering being an unrepentant villain, in this particular case, he maybe had to make an exception to his rule. Just this once.

"Come on!" he said, and took a running start and

dove into the water. It was cold, and he heard himself make a small, high-pitched bark that sounded like "Yipe!"

"Um, maybe I should wait here," Jack said, pacing nervously at the water's edge.

The Bad Hat ignored that, and started paddling out towards the person who was in danger.

He'd only gotten to swim that one time, long ago, but he was happy to see that he was good at it. His legs knew exactly what to do, and he noticed that when he used his tail, too, sweeping it back and forth, that he could move even faster.

"You can do it, Bad Hat!" Jack yelled.

The dog was concentrating so hard on the swimming, that he almost went right by the person.

It was an older man, who was gasping and choking and flailing.

"Glurp," the man said hoarsely.

Whatever. The details didn't really matter, at the moment.

The man was wearing bathing trunks and a thin shirt made of some kind of weird material. The Bad Hat thought it might be called neoprene? Either way, he experimentally tugged on the sleeve with his teeth, and was pleased to see that he could get a good, solid grip.

The man was so scared that he clutched at the Bad Hat's neck—and promptly pulled them both underwater.

Which really wasn't helpful.

The Bad Hat thrashed back up to the surface and coughed out most of the lake water he had just swallowed. Then, he stuck his muzzle in the water, fastened his teeth around the collar of the thick shirt, and started swimming towards the shore.

"Come on, Bad Hat!" Jack said, standing up on his hind legs and waving his front paws in the air. "I'm right over here!"

Very helpful. Although the current *was* pretty strong, so maybe it was good to have a furry landmark.

Wow, the man was heavy. And it was hard to keep both of their heads above the water. But, the Bad Hat churned steadily forward, dragging the man along next to him. Little waves kept splashing up, into the dog's face and nose—and he would have trouble breathing for a couple of seconds—but he kept his gaze on the shoreline and swam on without pausing.

It seemed to take forever, but finally, his paws scraped

against sand and rocks, and he stopped swimming, because he could walk from here.

The man was trying to stand up by himself, but couldn't seem to make his legs work right. So, the Bad Hat ignored his feeble attempts, and pulled him up onto the cement driveway. He gently deposited the man there, and then released the shirt from his teeth. It was good to be able to move his jaw freely again, and he shook off some of the water from his coat. Wow, that lake was *seriously* cold.

"I can take it from here," Jack said confidently, and nudged the man's face with one paw.

Whatever. The Bad Hat looked down at the man, who was coughing and exhausted, but didn't seem to be drowned or anything. In fact, he was trying to talk, even though he still couldn't quite catch his breath.

"Maybe we should go get some help," Jack said.

The Bad Hat snorted some more water out of his nostrils, and then sniffed the air. It smelled as though one of the nearby cottages might be occupied. "Over there," he said. "Let's go!"

So, they raced over to the house, stood outside the back door, and began barking.

After a while, the door opened and a woman stood there, holding a spatula.

Whoa, was she going to hit them with that? Just in case, the Bad Hat jumped back and out of the way.

Although the spatula smelled so deliciously of fried ham, that getting smacked with it might sting a lot less than it would have otherwise.

"Who are you two?" the woman asked, sounding curious.

Whoa. Totally existential question. The Bad Hat stopped barking to do a little inventory of his life, and the various problems he was grappling with—wait. There was a much more pressing issue. So, he went back to barking.

"Have you ever seen *Lassie*?" Jack asked. "*That's* what we need to do."

"Who's Lassie?" the Bad Hat asked.

Jack looked horrified. "You don't know who Lassie is? Bad Hat, you just failed on so many levels, that I don't even know how to—" He shook his head. "Watch and learn." He backed up a few feet across the lady's yard, barked, returned to her door, and then repeated the whole process, going further this time.

"What does that accomplish?" the Bad Hat asked.

"It'll make her follow us," Jack said, and did it again.

The woman looked around suspiciously. "Is this some kind of reality-show stunt? Because I really have no interest in being on television."

Well, the Bad Hat didn't, either, unless maybe someone wanted to buy the rights to his life story, and he had script approval and an executive-producer credit.

Regardless, he joined Jack in his run-away-come-back-run-away motion a few times.

"Where are your owners?" the woman asked.

The Bad Hat looked at Jack. "She's not very smart."

Jack shrugged. "Mostly, people aren't, as far as I know. We'll have to keep trying."

It felt like a waste of time, but because the Bad Hat had the steely-eyed patience of a saint, he kept running back and forth with Jack until the lady *finally* got the idea. She put down the spatula, took off her slippers, and stepped into a pair of untied hiking boots. Then, she followed them past two cottages, to the driveway where the man was still wheezing and trying to get up.

"Oh, no!" she said. "Vern, what happened?"

"Got a cramp while I was doing my swim," the man groaned. "But, your dogs saved me." Then, he paused. "You don't have a dog, Margie."

"No, I don't," the woman agreed, fishing a cell phone out of the pocket of her sweatpants.

"No, please, I'm fine," the man protested, as she called for an ambulance.

"Hush, Vern," she said. "We need to have the paramedics come and check you out, to be sure."

"We saved him!" Jack barked proudly to the Bad Hat. "We're like heroes!"

"What 'we,' little man?" the Bad Hat asked.

Jack just strutted around, giving the man an encouraging pat with his paw every so often.

"Whose dogs are these?" Vern asked. He was sitting up now, but still looking pale. "I can't think of anyone on Whittemore Point who owns dogs like these."

No one was *ever* going to *own* the Bad Hat. Oh, no. Not happening.

"See if you can catch them," Vern said. "We need to make sure that they get home safely."

Margie nodded and reached for the Bad Hat—who dodged adroitly out of the way. Then, she tried to pick up Jack, who leaped gracefully and spun away from her. She kept trying to corral them, and the dogs found it childishly easy to elude her—repeatedly. In fact, it was an

113

entertaining game, and the Bad Hat was enjoying himself.

"This is fun!" Jack said.

The Bad Hat totally agreed.

The chase went on for a little while longer, until Margie finally stopped, out of breath.

"Come here, boys," Margie said, holding out a friendly hand for them to sniff. "No one's going to hurt you. We just want to get you home."

Never happen. Although the Bad Hat thought of a possible backup plan. "She smells like breakfast meat," he said. "Maybe we should let her catch us, just long enough to have some food, and then we can escape again."

Jack hesitated—which gave Margie a chance to scoop him up into her arms.

"Oh, wow," Jack said, as she swooped him into the air. "That wasn't supposed to happen."

"Want me to knock her down?" the Bad Hat asked, poised to leap.

Jack frowned. "I don't know. Maybe she would be a good owner for us. This could be our new home."

When was he going to grasp that the Bad Hat didn't want a home? He was his *own* home. Complete independence was like, the hallmark of his creed.

"What a good boy," Margie said, stroking Jack's head. "Can you help me catch your friend?"

Jack grinned wickedly at the Bad Hat, who gave him a very evil look in return.

Just then, they heard sirens, and an ambulance and a police car showed up.

"That's our cue, little man," the Bad Hat said.

"To do what?" Jack asked.

"To get out of here already," the Bad Hat said. "We're lawless creatures, who run with the wind."

"She has *ham* in that house, with our names on it," Jack said.

Which was a good point, but it was still time to go. "Sorry, I'm out of here," the Bad Hat said. "You'd better pitch a fit or something, or else I'm going to leave you behind."

Jack sighed, but then began writhing and shrieking and twisting, until Margie had no *choice*, but to drop him.

"You owe me some ham," he said, when he landed on the driveway.

"Put it on my tab," the Bad Hat said.

They wagged their tails at Margie and Vern, and then darted into the woods and out of sight.

"Thank you!" Vern called after them.

"You're welcome!" Jack barked back.

That was all well and good, but the dog was the *Bad Hat*. He did not require thanks. Freedom was his only reward.

Was there a song in that? Or, at least, an epic poem? Probably.

"We were so brave," Jack said.

"Yeah, it was amazing, the way you gave instructions," the Bad Hat said.

Jack puffed his chest out. "No need to thank me. I was happy to help."

The Bad Hat was a little tired from his swim, but the water had been refreshing. Maybe he would have to make a point of stopping by the lake every day for a quick dip, and then, a long rest on one of the rocky beaches.

"Let's go around the whole lake, and get the lay of the land," the Bad Hat said, as they trotted down a mostly deserted dirt road.

Jack shook his head. "My paws are pretty tired. Could we just go back now, and maybe take naps? I'm sort of weary."

Naturally. "Hey, you can go back whenever you want," the Bad Hat said.

"Not me," Jack said. *"We."*

The Bad Hat paid no attention to that, ranging away from the lake, and onto paved roads, while Jack did his best to keep up.

Some of the houses were occupied, while others were closed up for the season. The town seemed to be a combination of farms, rental cabins, fancy houses, vacation homes, and cottages. It was already September, so most of the tourists must have gone home, because things seemed pretty quiet.

Jack let out a wistful sigh. "I bet everyone's running in the meadow, while Monica gets our lunch ready."

Probably, yeah. And some lunch would be nice. Too bad the Bad Hat was never going to go back there.

At a house up ahead, he could see a man and a woman fondly saying good-bye to each other. That was unusual, in his world. There hadn't been too many hugs at any of the homes where he had lived.

"Check it out," he said. "Those people *like* each other."

Jack's eyes lit up. "They look nice. Maybe they would make us some lunch!"

In the front yard, a toddler was playing around on the grass with a brightly colored plastic beach ball.

"Oooh, a toy!" Jack said, and scampered over to join the child.

The Bad Hat wasn't about to interact with any more people, but he *loved* to play with balls. Jack pushed the ball towards the girl with his nose—and then, she pushed it back. It looked fun! Really fun!

Once, the mean family who had adopted him had had a ball that looked like that. The dog had been so excited that he jumped on it—and it popped. Loudly.

The noise scared him, and the mother yelled at him for wrecking the ball—and, well, it had been another terrible day, in a long series of terrible days.

So, the dog had learned his lesson and would leave this ball alone. But, that didn't mean that he couldn't stand here, and watch, and imagine that he was being allowed to play, too. Seemed like a harmless little fantasy.

The woman was waving as she got into a white minivan, and the man waved back at her, as he headed towards the lawn. But, just as she started to back out of the driveway, the ball rolled away from Jack and the toddler, who both chased after it.

Right behind the moving car!

There was no time to make a plan or hesitate, so the

Bad Hat just sprang into action and tore across the road.

"Wendy, no!" the man said, sounding terrified. "Rhoda, stop the car!"

He was running towards the child, but the Bad Hat could see that he wasn't going to make it in time. So, the dog ran even faster.

"What's going on?" Jack asked, looking confused.

The dog head-butted him as hard as he could, and Jack catapulted through the air, away from the car. Then, the Bad Hat focused on the little girl. He was going to grab her arm, but was afraid he might bite her, by mistake. So, he dug his teeth into the back of the little girl's waistband and jerked her up off the driveway in one clean motion.

It was hard to leap with about thirty pounds hanging from his muzzle, but the dog did his best. He felt the metal bumper of the car scrape painfully across his sore ribs—ow!—as he sailed over to the safety of the grass.

They landed hard, but the dog twisted at the last second, so that the little girl would fall on top of him, instead of the ground.

There was a frightening explosive sound as the back wheels of the car ran over the beach ball, and the dog cringed instinctively. Then, there was the screech of brakes, and the car stopped, a couple of inches away from his tail and left hind leg.

Whew. That had been *close.*

"Wow," Jack gasped. "Are you all right?"

It had all happened so quickly, that the Bad Hat wasn't even sure how he felt. Shaken up, mostly.

But, was the little girl okay? Well, probably, since she was laughing and clapping her hands and shouting, "Funny! Funny!"

The grown-ups were both yelling, their voices so frantic that he couldn't quite understand what they were saying, and the dog swiftly boosted the toddler up to her feet. Then, he warily sidled away, in case the parents were going to kick him or something. But, instead, they started hugging the little girl, everyone jabbering at once, and no one even seemed to notice him.

Okay, good. It was better that way.

He retreated back across the road, and sat down for a moment, to catch his breath. Wow, he had never run that fast before. It felt like he had maybe scraped the pads on one of his front paws, which hurt. But, he would wait until he was sure he was out of public view to lick the injury mournfully, and feel very, very sorry for himself.

In the meantime, Jack was nuzzling the little girl's face, and she gave him a big kiss in return.

"Whose dog is that?" the woman asked.

"I don't know," the man said. "But, he saved Wendy's life."

Seriously? The Bad Hat wasn't sure whether to laugh— or be outraged.

The parents patted Jack lavishly, and the Bad Hat couldn't help being amused, as he watched him enjoying all of the attention and affection.

"Thank God. I'm so sorry. I—I'll never—" The woman stopped, shaking her head. Then, she stood up, and snapped her fingers invitingly. "Come here, boy. Let's get you home."

Jack wagged his tail enthusiastically, but stayed just out of reach. "Should I let her? To see if we can get some lunch out of it?"

Was every single person they ever met in New Hampshire going to be determined to rescue them? He was the Bad Hat. Bad Hats never needed rescuing, or intervention. A simple nod of respect, and perhaps a brief wave, was all he requested.

"Up to you, little man," he said. "But, I'm hitting the road."

Jack sighed, but then ran after him. "Wait for me!"

They traveled down the road at a steady trot. Sometimes, they were on damp dirt roads; sometimes, they were on pavement. The dirt roads certainly felt a lot better on the Bad Hat's paws—one of which *was* scraped, and he was planning to allow himself a solid ten minutes of glum self-pity and moping about the small wound, as soon as he got a chance.

"Thank you for helping out," Jack said.

Helping out? The Bad Hat just looked at him.

"Okay," Jack said, and grinned at him. "Thank you for saving me."

Better. Much better. "You're welcome," the Bad Hat said.

CHAPTER EIGHT

They ran around unfamiliar roads for what seemed like a long time.

"This is nice and all," Jack said, after a while, "but I'm really tired."

That made two of them.

"Can we go home?" Jack asked. "And sneak out again, after we eat, and maybe rest a little?"

No, no, and *no*. This was supposed to be a nonstop, glorious, wildly eventful series of adventures. So, the Bad Hat shook his head.

Jack sighed. "Okay. I love you like a brother, Bad Hat, but I'm *starving*. I'll try to come back later."

With that, he turned to go.

Wait, just like that? "Um, you're going to leave me?" the Bad Hat said. "By myself?"

"It's lunchtime," Jack said. "I need my nourishment. See you soon!"

As he galloped away, the Bad Hat could hear him shouting at the top of his lungs, "Gravy, gravy, gravy! Lots and lots of gravy! I can't wait to have some very delicious gravy!"

When Jack disappeared around a curve in the road, the Bad Hat couldn't help feeling a little sad and lonely. But, even though the compatriot system was sort of nice, it wasn't like he didn't know how to be by himself. And he preferred it that way!

So, the dog continued down the road, trying not to let his tail drag on the ground. Because he wasn't sad. Nope. He was happy. He *loved* being a loner. Every single moment of his life was magical!

He was only trudging because he had hurt his foot, and didn't want to put too much weight on it, that's all.

And he *wasn't* upset about not getting to have any gravy.

As he limped along, *enjoying every single second* of his total isolation from the rest of the world, his delightful silence was suddenly broken by about a trillion voices all shouting at once.

Or, anyway, at least a couple of hundred.

All he knew for sure was that it was a school of some kind. Children often looked alike to him—mostly because not many kids had ever been nice to him, and so, he had learned to ignore them as much as possible.

These particular children seemed to be about twelve years old, maybe. The playground was crowded, and noisy, and there were balls of various kinds being hurled around. Footballs, baseballs, soccer balls, basketballs, red kickballs, and even two girls playing catch with lacrosse sticks and a tiny hard rubber ball.

The Bad Hat stared, with his mouth hanging open in wonder. Balls! So many balls! Wow!

Most of the kids were playing games, although some were sitting in small groups and talking. A few others were by themselves, staring at electronic devices. The Bad Hat had never been able to figure out the complete fascination people seemed to feel for their silly gadgets. Whether they were walking, or in cars, or sitting down, so many of them gazed at ridiculous little gizmos nonstop. Such a waste of time, in his opinion.

Unless they were watching movies on the devices. Then, maybe, it was okay.

He really wanted to chase after some of the balls, and maybe even play fetch—but, he didn't want to risk having anyone be mean to him. So, he watched the children intently to see if any of them were eating snacks. After all, he was terribly hungry, and it would be easy enough to swoop by and snatch granola bars and cookies and whatever else *right out of their little hands.*

It would be funny, too.

But, mean. And it wouldn't be right for a cowboy-like revered icon to be mean. It might even be too mean for the average *villain* who wasn't fit to be seen in polite society. Maybe, though, if he was lucky, someone nearby would drop part of what he or she was eating. Everyone knew that *all* dropped food belonged to dogs. Always had, always would.

He noticed a scruffy little boy standing near the sidelines of a touch football game. It was clear that he wanted to play, but was either too shy to ask or was waiting for someone to invite him.

The kid had rumpled brown hair, wire-framed glasses, a half-untucked shirt, and blue jeans that were too short for him. One of his sneakers was untied, too.

All in all, he looked like the kind of kid who ate paste.

Not that the Bad Hat didn't enjoy some unconventional snacks himself—but, he drew the line at paste.

In fact, all the kid needed was a KICK ME REALLY HARD! sign on his back, and he could be the dictionary definition of a walking target.

But, did he have any food? If he had food, he would be an easy mark. But—oh, yeah—stealing food was mean.

Too bad. The dog was starving.

Except, wait, the kid was pulling something out of his pocket. It was wrapped in plastic. Could it be—yes! *Beef jerky!* Which was only the very best food in the entire world.

The Bad Hat gave him a chance to unwrap it—since plastic tasted awful—and then swept past him, snatching the jerky away.

"Hey!" the kid protested. Then, he shrugged. "Okay," he said, and took out another piece of plastic-wrapped jerky, which he opened and began to chew.

If the boy had two pieces, it wasn't stealing. It was *sharing.* And sharing was a nice thing to do.

The Bad Hat gulped down his piece of beef jerky in seconds, and then looked at the kid, who had only managed to gnaw away about a third of his piece. So, the Bad Hat cocked his head to one side, in an attempt to look as cute as possible.

Nope, the kid was still chewing.

So, the dog raised both of his front paws in the air. Some might call that begging, but when it came to beef jerky, there was no such thing as dignity.

The kid laughed. "Okay, you win," he said, and tossed the rest of it over.

Yes! The Bad Hat caught the meat effortlessly. It might not be gravy, but it was still mighty good.

Three boys from the football game came swaggering over to the kid with glasses—who, judging from his welcoming smile, was naive enough to think that they were being friendly. But, as far as the Bad Hat could tell, Paste Kid was definitely in some trouble here.

"How's it going?" Paste Kid asked, still smiling.

"Bet you wish you could play," one of the boys said. He was one of those hulking, unwieldy kids with really big feet, who hadn't grown into his height yet.

"Sure," Paste Kid said. "I mean, if you need an extra guy."

The Bad Hat nodded approvingly. Apparently, the kid had at least a shred of cool. Knew enough not to sound too eager, and to keep his response vague and open-ended.

"What, you think we want some little wishes-he-was-Harry-Potter twerp out there?" one of the other jocks said, and he and his friends laughed.

Paste Kid blushed, straightened his glasses, and blushed again. "I have amblyopia," he muttered. "That's why I need the glasses."

The Bad Hat wanted to groan. The kid had had the high ground—and he'd blushed himself right back into being a victim.

"Well, let's see how tough you are," a boy wearing a Bruins hat said, and then shoved Paste Kid as hard as he could.

The kid went flying, landing flat on his back in the mud, losing his glasses along the way.

Whoa! Not good. Not good at all. The Bad Hat watched alertly, trying to decide whether it was time to intercede.

Bruins Punk laughed. "Did that hurt?"

"N-no," Paste Kid said shakily, as he fumbled for his glasses, but couldn't find them.

The Bad Hat gave him a B-minus for that. An A for pluck, but a D for letting his voice tremble.

As Paste Kid started to get up, one of the punks pushed him right back down again.

"Did *that* hurt?" one of the other bullies asked, laughing.

"Nope," Paste Kid said, lying in the mud.

Okay, another B-minus. A for sounding brave. D-plus for not getting up right away.

But, it was starting to look as though the confrontation was going to move from insults and pushing to actual pummeling. And the Bad Hat did not approve of pummeling. So, he strode purposefully over to the group of boys, and used his muzzle to poke Paste Kid in the back.

The kid twisted around to see who else was attacking him, and then squinted at him fuzzily. "Oh, it's just you," he said, sounding surprised.

Well, how about *Yay! Thank you! A very noble canine has raced to save me!*? The Bad Hat nudged him more forcefully, to try and urge him up to his feet. But, the kid seemed to be confused, and just sat there looking at him.

"That your dog?" one of the bullies asked. "He looks dumb."

Dumb? Someone was calling him *dumb*? The Bad Hat

most assuredly did not cotton to that. No, sir, he did not.

"He's not dumb," Paste Kid said, climbing to his feet. "I think *you* guys are dumb."

All right, the kid had heart! The dog definitely approved. Not much originality, or the gift of clever retorts—but, heart!

The bullies apparently decided that that was a good enough reason to start a fistfight, and one of them threw a punch and hit Paste Kid right in the face. Paste Kid staggered back, clearly stunned.

Nope. Not on his watch. The dog quickly jumped in between Paste Kid and the other three boys. He gave the bullies a long, ominous stare—and they all stopped short, with their fists drawn back.

"Hey, call your dog off," one of them said uneasily.

"He's not—" Paste Kid paused. "I mean, I think he just wants you guys to leave me alone."

Yep. He'd have to give that answer an A. The dog blinked at the bullies—once.

Which seemed to scare them. So, he did it again.

"He'd better not bite me," the boy in the Bruins cap said. "My parents will totally sue you, if he bites me."

The Bad Hat found that insulting. He never bit

anyone—not even people who kicked or hit him. Shoot, he didn't even growl at anyone.

Unless they *really* got on his nerves.

"Hey, what's going on over there?" a voice asked.

An adult. Finally. The Bad Hat had been wondering why teachers hadn't noticed that some poor kid was getting shoved around.

"Jake's trying to get his dog to bite me!" the boy in the Bruins cap shouted. "He—"

The Bad Hat moved so that his shoulder barely brushed against the Bruins punk's leg—and then he fell down onto his side, yelping and whimpering, and holding up his right front paw limply.

The teacher looked shocked. "Bruce, did you just kick that dog?"

"No!" Bruce said defensively. "He was trying to knock me over, and—and well, I didn't do anything!"

Imagining how Jack would react to this, the Bad Hat whimpered even more pitifully and tried to stand up. Then, he pretended that his paw wouldn't hold his weight, and collapsed to the ground.

"I can't believe you would deliberately injure a beautiful animal like that," the teacher said sternly.

"I didn't!" But, Bruce was starting to look unsure of himself, as the Bad Hat let out another sad moan and let his head slump into the mud. "I mean, maybe my foot slipped a little, or—"

The teacher glared at him. "In other words, you kicked the poor dog."

"Well, um—" Bruce frowned. "I don't know."

The Bad Hat was having a *very* hard time not showing how amused he was by all of this.

"I've heard enough," their teacher said, her voice brisk. "Bruce, I want you to march down to the office, and wait for me to get there." She turned towards Paste Kid. "Were these three picking on you, Jake?"

Paste Kid hesitated. "Well—"

Whoa, a lot on the line here. The Bad Hat watched, his supposedly mangled paw still up in the air. Would the kid rat out the three jerks? Which might help—but, might also make things worse. And from the way the bullies were glaring at the kid, the Bad Hat was guessing *worse* was the way it would go, in this case.

"We had a confrontation, but everything's under control now," Paste Kid said. "I think we came to an understanding, and we aren't going to have any more problems."

Really? Maybe the Bad Hat's instincts weren't any good, but that wasn't what *he* thought would happen.

The teacher didn't seem to buy it, either, but she nodded. "All right. But if there are *any* problems, I want to hear about it right away. We have zero tolerance for bullying here." She frowned at the kid in the Bruins cap. "Bruce, I don't see you marching to the office. Let's go! Kyle and Roger, I'll be keeping a *very* close eye on you two from now on. And Jake, why don't you call your par—" She stopped. "Um, your mother, that is, and have her come and pick up your dog."

As she went off with the Bruins creep, one of the other bullies leaned close to Jake.

"This isn't over," he said. "And you'd better not fink on us."

Jake looked right back at him. "Someday, when I own a huge tech company, you two are going to show up begging for jobs—*and I'm not going to hire you.*"

Which left both bullies speechless.

The Bad Hat wanted to laugh, but he decided just to cradle his paw, and milk his imaginary injury a little more, instead.

After the two bullies had slogged off, grumbling and embarrassed, Jake looked over at the Bad Hat.

"I don't think he kicked you," he said. "You're a total faker."

Naturally, the dog didn't respond, but he *did* spring effortlessly to his feet.

Jake nodded. "I thought so. You're a good actor, though."

Yes, down the road, that skill would help contribute to the Legend of the Bad Hat. In fact, he was probably going to need a theme song, too. Something catchy, and memorable. And maybe a viral video or two.

In the meantime, Paste Kid was still sitting in the mud. So, the dog fastened his teeth into the kid's shirt collar and yanked him up to his feet.

There was a distinct ripping sound, and they both froze.

"Don't worry," Jake said. "I always rip my shirts by accident. Mom's used to it."

So, she was probably, reluctantly, used to him eating paste, too.

"Let's see your paw," Jake said.

The Bad Hat lifted his paw without thinking, and the boy examined his right front leg carefully. To the dog's surprise, he seemed to know what he was doing—his hands felt like a veterinarian's hands.

"Okay, good," Jake said, and put his paw down. "I

was almost sure you were faking, but, just in case."

His other front paw *did* hurt, from getting scraped earlier, but the dog was much too self-reliant to show him that, of course. Although it was tempting.

When the kid reached out to pat him, the Bad Hat instinctively flinched away.

"Uh, sorry," Jake said, and pulled his hand back. "I wonder if you live around here? Your owners are going to be worried."

As if. The Bad Hat was as free and independent as autumn leaves drifting in the evening breeze, by God. But, the important question was, did the kid have any more jerky hidden away? He sniffed carefully, but apparently, it was all gone.

Which was *so* disappointing.

"You must have gotten lost," Jake said. "I need to find a way to get you home. Come on, I'll take you down to the—"

Again, with the rescuing? New Hampshire people were truly freaky. The dog turned abruptly and galloped towards the woods.

"Hey, wait!" Jake called. "Come back!"

The Bad Hat just kept running.

CHAPTER NINE

Two pieces of beef jerky did not a nutritious lunch make, but at least it had taken the edge off his appetite. So, maybe he wouldn't collapse, or faint, or anything like that. Not for a while yet.

Next time, he should probably figure out a way to bring snacks *with* him. Maybe Florence and the other cats could rig up some sort of saddlebag for him, or— well, not that he was going to see the cats ever again.

Because he wasn't ever going to go back there.

Probably.

Unless it was just to say hi.

For a minute.

Because he definitely did not miss anyone, especially

not Jack, and he wasn't homesick. He *liked* his solitary journey. It was his dream come true.

Yep. That was his story, and he was sticking to it.

As he walked along, he saw some shops constructed with old red bricks, a gas station, and a couple of homey-looking restaurants with curtains in the windows and geraniums on the porches. There was an old wooden bridge up ahead, and he crossed it carefully, seeing a fast-rushing river below. The water didn't seem to be very deep, because there were lots of big granite rocks sticking out, with waves splashing and bubbling up against them. He peered down at the water, able to see small fish darting about in the less choppy areas.

Could he catch fish to eat? More to the point, did he *want* to catch fish to eat? Not really. Yeah, he was hungry, but maybe not *that* hungry.

So, the Bad Hat followed a curvy, tree-shaded road into what seemed to be the center of town. Wait, maybe this was the village green, where the adoption fairs were held? All of the buildings were painted white, and looked old, and were arranged neatly around a grassy common area. There was a church with a tall steeple, a quaint little post office, a general store combined with a small diner, a town hall, a library, and a public-safety building, with a fire truck and two police cars parked in front of it. Across the common, there were about six colonial-style white houses with black shutters. The common itself had trees, and park benches, a few war memorials and statues, a flagpole with an American flag snapping back and forth in the wind, and an old-fashioned bandstand.

Yes, he was a proud Southern boy—but, he had to admit that New England was very scenic.

It was warm and sunny, and he wanted to go roll in the grass for a while. Unfortunately, there were people around, strolling in the park and doing errands, and his being out in the open would not be at all inconspicuous.

The little restaurant smelled good—bacon! hamburgers! fried chicken!—and he decided that he would explore behind the building. Maybe they would have some garbage cans sitting right there, full of tasty scraps, just *waiting* for him to wander by and help himself.

He thought it might be fun to pretend that he was a spy, trying to escape from rogue agents and make his way to safe—or, at least, neutral—territory. So, the Bad Hat slunk around the side of the building, staying so low to the ground that he was almost crawling. He hid behind trees, and stayed in the shadows. Then, whenever he came to an open area, he would crouch down, count to three—and dash towards the next shadow.

Oh, he was sly. Really sly. The CIA only *wished* that he would apply to join them.

He bent down and prepared to knock the trash can over with admirable grace and efficiency. But, just as he was about to jump, he heard a noise behind him—and stopped in his tracks.

Duke ran up to him, panting heavily. "Wow, I'm really glad I found you. It was awful—it took almost twenty minutes! I'm *so tired*."

Well, he wasn't very good at hiding, if he could be discovered that quickly by yet another colleague. "Why did you come after me?" the Bad Hat asked. "I already sent Jack away." Well, sort of. "I'm a renegade, off to strike my fortune and make my way in the world."

Duke looked puzzled. "What does that mean?"

So much for German Shepherds supposedly being way smarter than all other dogs. "I'm like a fugitive, Duke," the Bad Hat said. "So, no one's supposed to be able to find me."

"Oh." Duke frowned. "Sorry about that. But, Florence is really mad and says you need to come home right away."

That was predictable. Cats thought they were in charge of absolutely everything. "It's an animal-rescue shelter," the Bad Hat said. "Not a home."

"I don't know about that. I like it there very much," Duke said. "Anyway, she says that, um—well, you know, the *people* are very upset, and that she won't stand for that."

Probably a direct quote, except for the vague part. And the lack of a stamping paw.

"The people have been—" Duke paused. "I forget. What are their names again?"

He had to be kidding. "Seriously?" the Bad Hat said.

Duke nodded, his expression guileless and innocent.

"Oh, dude, that is so sad," the Bad Hat said.

"*Duke,*" Duke corrected him. "It's okay, it's an easy mistake to make."

Very, very sad. Pathetic, even. And Duke was clearly an expert when it came to making mistakes. No wonder he had been downgraded. "Joan and Thomas are the main ones," the Bad Hat said. "They live in the house.

And Monica cooks for us. Sometimes, other volunteers come, too, to help out."

"Really?" Duke gave that some thought. "Okay, that sounds about right. Thanks, Webster."

Oh, so *that* name he remembered?

"You're going to come back now, right?" Duke said.

The Bad Hat shook his head. "No. I'm too busy having adventures and stuff. But, say hi to everyone for me."

"I'm supposed to tell you how worried they all are," Duke said. "There was another dog missing, too, this morning, but I think that one is home already."

The Bad Hat nodded. "Right. That's Jack."

Duke looked baffled. "Which one is Jack? Does he take us out to the meadow?"

The Bad Hat wasn't sure whether to laugh or groan. "Jack's the Yorkshire Terrier. The little one everyone really likes, even though he barks a lot."

Duke thought some more. Then, his eyes brightened. "The brown one! Who hates to get his claws clipped! Oh, yes, I like him, too. He's just *swell*."

Swell. He hadn't heard *that* one recently. Gosh. Gee. Golly. "So, make sure to say a special hello for me, and tell him that I hope he had a good lunch, but he missed out on some beef jerky," the Bad Hat said.

"That's a lot to remember," Duke said, looking worried. "And Florence'll be, you know, cross. You should really come with me, instead, so she can stop fretting about you."

How had he found himself in a world where it actually bothered him that some cat might be upset? The Bad Hat sighed. "Look, buddy," he started.

"*Duke,*" Duke said kindly. "It's okay. Names are hard for me, too."

Duke might be a simple tool, but to his credit, he was sweet about it. "Duke, the problem is that I have more thrilling exploits planned for today," the Bad Hat said. Not that he could think of any, at the moment, but he was positively *sure* that they would take place. "Tell her if she can leave a gate ajar, or a door or a window open, I'll come by after midnight, and check in for a minute, okay?"

"I don't know," Duke said doubtfully. "She's going to be really mad at me, if I show up alone."

The Bad Hat shrugged. "It's the best I can do, big fella."

"*Duke,*" Duke said. "If you think of something that

begins with *D*, and picture it whenever you see me, that might make it easier." He paused. "If you can think of something that begins with *D*, that is."

"Dog," the Bad Hat said.

Duke nodded happily. "Dog! Yes, that's a good one! Thank you! Anyway, I'll tell Florence to—what?"

If only he had a pen and paper—and knew how to write—so that he could just send her a note directly. "Leave a door or something open," the Bad Hat said. "So I can sneak in tonight."

"That's right, now I remember," Duke said. "All right, I'll tell her, but if she yells at me, I'll have to blame you completely, okay?"

The idea of facing the Wrath of Florence was not appealing. "You could tell her you couldn't find me?" the Bad Hat suggested.

Duke gave him a scornful look. "No one would believe that, Webster. I'm a *police dog*."

Scary thought. Duke, with the power to detain, arrest, Mirandize, and interrogate. "Look, I promise I'll show up tonight," the Bad Hat said. "I won't be able to stay long—you know, on account of my exhilarating shenanigans, and my vision quest—but, I *will* stop by."

"Vision quest," Duke repeated, sounding uncertain. "Wow, this is *so hard.* And I'm very confused. I'm going home now, okay?"

"Okay," the Bad Hat said. Was it safe to let this poor guy walk anyplace by himself? "Be careful when you cross streets. Make sure to look both ways."

Duke nodded. "That's what Florence told me, too. But, I forget why."

Sometimes, it was hard not to be speechless around Duke. "To see if any cars are coming," the Bad Hat said. "So that you can avoid them, and you won't get hurt."

Duke looked relieved. "Right! Now I remember. Thanks, Mad Cap!"

Close enough. "Just be careful," the Bad Hat said.

"You, too," Duke said. Then, he looked both ways— more than once, cautiously crossed the quiet street, and raced off.

The Bad Hat's plan was to have an insanely exciting afternoon, but in the end, he just tipped over a trash can and ate a bunch of leftovers from the restaurant. Cold scrambled eggs, part of a tuna fish sandwich, some limp French fries, discarded garden salad, and—best of all!— most of a piece of meat loaf.

When he was finished, there was such a mess on the ground that he wondered whether he'd be breaking the Bad Hat code, if he cleaned it up. Although it would be better not to leave any clues behind, right? So, he used his muzzle to shove most of the nonedible trash back into the can. Then, with a strong flip of his paw, he pushed the can upright again, exactly where it had been. Now, there would be no obvious forensic evidence remaining to reveal his antisocial criminal act.

Oh, he was an *excellent* spy. So furtive, so clever.

Pleasantly full of the remains of people's lunches, he took a long nap on the floor of the bandstand. The weathered wooden floor wasn't incredibly comfortable, but he was less visible to the outside world than he would have been if he had flopped down on the grass in the late-afternoon sun.

Even though it was dark now, it had to be at least several hours until midnight, and so, unless some new and glorious experiences came his way, he had a lot of time to kill. Fortunately, he was equipped with vast inner resources, and knew exactly what to do: curl up and take another nap.

When he woke up, he had no idea what time it was.

But, he yawned and stretched in a nice, leisurely way. It was maybe too cold outside, but other than that, he had had a very comfortable rest.

Whew, he sure hoped they were having a viewing party tonight. He was *hungry*.

Was it midnight yet? Close enough. Besides, it would take him a while to find his way back to the rescue farm.

He made a couple of wrong turns—which he would never, ever admit to anyone—but soon, he was standing in the woods, observing the house, the kennels, the barn, and the meadow. It was too cloudy for there to be any moonlight, but the house was dark and quiet, and he assumed that Joan and Thomas were asleep.

Maybe it was later than midnight? And he had wasted some prime snacking and viewing time? That would be terrible.

He tried to leap over the fence into the meadow. Unfortunately, he mistimed his jump and fell a little short. But, he was able to scrabble over the top, and landed in the grass with a thump.

Ow.

Good thing he was alone, and no one had seen that happen, or he would be mortified.

"Nice one, dog," a voice above him said. "Really smooth."

The Bad Hat looked up, and saw an owl sitting on a branch in a nearby maple tree, laughing his round head off.

"Just trying to entertain you," the Bad Hat said, attempting to recover his dignity.

"Great job!" the owl said, and laughed some more. Then, he scrutinized the dog carefully. "You probably weigh about seventy-five pounds, right?"

Thereabouts. More like ninety, if he was getting regular meals. "Yeah," the dog said.

The owl sighed. "Too bad. Even if the hawks came and helped, you're too big for us to carry off for supper."

What? The dog's mouth fell open in total horror.

The owl laughed even harder. "Just kidding. I went vegetarian a couple of years ago." He frowned. "Getting kind of tired of nuts and seeds, I have to say."

It would take a huge *flock* of owls and hawks to have any hope of hauling him away, but the dog still wanted to throw up. Especially because he didn't care for heights, and the idea of flying held no appeal at all. "Sounds like a good lifestyle change, though," the Bad Hat said.

The owl shrugged. "I was cruising around, and I

ended up hanging out near a monastery for a few weeks. So, now it's all 'do no harm' and 'be considerate' for me." He let out another sigh. "But sometimes, I miss being a predator."

An owl with *angst*, of all things.

The owl flew down to perch on top of the fence. "My sister says it would be okay just to eat insects and worms. What do you think?"

This conversation was way over his head. Outlaws didn't spend much time studying philosophy or ethics. "Um, well," the dog said, "I don't know. I guess it's better than chomping on things like baby bunnies. But, insects and worms are alive, too, even though they aren't, you know, *cute*, and possibly not, um, sentient. So, maybe it's—complicated?"

The owl blinked slowly. "Unlike the average canine, you seem to be a little bit wise."

The Bad Hat really hated being patronized by random wildlife. "Yeah. Me smart for dog," he said stiffly.

The owl laughed. "Oooh, he's touchy."

Yeah, yeah, yeah. "Enjoy your nuts and seeds," the Bad Hat said. "Maybe you can have some roots and tubers, too."

"Yum," the owl said, without much enthusiasm.

After saying good night, the dog galloped across the

meadow. As always, it felt good to stretch his legs. And, with no Greyhound mixes or other ringers around, he could tell himself that he was unusually speedy, with fabulous first-step acceleration, which was the envy of all other dogs.

He could see that the damaged part of his former kennel had been repaired, and that the fallen tree had been cleared away. Apparently, the remains were being chopped up for winter firewood, based upon the pile of newly split logs next to what was left of the tree.

The main door leading out to the meadow was probably going to be the one left open for him, although there was no guarantee that Duke had managed to remember any of his instructions correctly. But, he could see a sliver of light, so apparently, some version of the message had gotten through.

Just as he started to nose the door open, it crossed his mind that it might be a trap, and he would be lured back into his kennel and never have a chance to escape again.

And that would be bad.

So, he backed off and paced nervously inside the meadow for a few minutes, trying to decide what to do. Should he just dash away? It would certainly be safer.

He could go back into the woods, make a bed on some pine needles, and get a chilly night's rest.

On the other hand, it wasn't like they were all missing him so much that life was no longer worth living, and they would be desperate to have him stay. They would probably just be happy to have him stop by to say hello, eat some kibble, and be on his jolly way.

Kibble. Having some kibble would be so completely excellent right about now.

And if they were going to watch more *Masterpiece Classic*, he really didn't want to miss it.

Okay. That tipped the balance.

He pushed tentatively at the door with his nose, and nudged his way inside.

"Well, finally!" a voice said.

A British accent. Florence.

"And what do you have to say for yourself?" she asked, tapping a paw testily on the floor. "Joan and Thomas have been beside themselves with worry."

Did they like him that much? Hard to believe. "Um, that I'm powerless to change the tides of my destiny," he said.

"Balderdash," Florence said.

That was another interpretation, yeah. "What do you want from me?" the dog asked. "I'm *bad*."

151

"I don't know about that, but you are certainly obsti-nate," Florence said. "And rather willful."

Probably. "I'm also really hungry," he said.

Florence looked at him with critical, crooked eyes. Then, she turned around clumsily and began stumping down the hall. "Very well," she said. "Follow me."

Didn't have to ask *him* twice. "Keep in mind, I'm only stopping by," the Bad Hat said, as he trailed behind her. "I'll be on my way after I say hello to everyone."

"Oh, no doubt," Florence agreed. "I daresay you won't even pause to have anything to eat before you go."

What a cruel and awful thought. "I might have a few bites," the Bad Hat said. "Just to be polite."

Florence nodded. "And I'm sure you won't want to stick around to see a movie, or anything of that nature, either."

She was really boxing him into an uncomfortable corner, wasn't she? "Well, if you think it would be good manners, I will," he said. "But, that's *it*. After that, I am gone, for good. You can count on that."

Florence smiled. "If you say so."

He did. *Emphatically.*

More or less.

CHAPTER TEN

They went straight to the den, which was crowded with animals, eating and chatting and looking cheerful.

"If it isn't Wayward Webster, the Prodigal Punk," Benjamin said.

"You're back!" Duke said happily.

Yep. Here he was. "Hi, Benjamin," the Bad Hat said. "Hi, Duke."

Duke shook his head. "No, I'm Marquess now."

Seriously? The Bad Hat turned to stare at Florence. "You demoted him? Why?"

"He didn't bring you home with him," Florence said. "That was his assignment, and he failed to complete it."

"Well, I'm here now," the Bad Hat said. "Doesn't that count?"

Florence delicately nibbled a piece of kibble, taking her own sweet time, before answering. "I'll think about it."

"That's really mean," the Bad Hat said. "You're like, evil to the core."

Florence shrugged, her expression not even remotely perturbed. "I'm a *cat.*"

Well, yeah, that pretty much spoke for itself, didn't it. "He made some very good arguments," the Bad Hat said. "It's not his fault that I'm, you know, incorrigible."

"True," Florence agreed, "but what am I going to do, start calling you the *Really* Bad Hat?"

Hmmm, he sort of liked that. It maybe even capture his, you know, essence. But, it didn't exactly come tripping lightly off the tongue, did it?

The Bad Hat turned back to Duke. "Marquess, you've just been upgraded. You're Duke again."

Duke's eyes glistened with tears. "Really? You wouldn't joke about a thing like that, would you?"

"Nope, I'm a dog, we don't play the game that way," the Bad Hat said. "You have officially been promoted."

"Oh my goodness," Duke said, sounding as though he was completely overcome. "Wow. This is wonderful news. Glorious news! I have *so many* animals to thank."

Everyone in the room turned, cooperatively, to look at him.

"Where to begin? Well, I never met my father," Duke said. "But, I'm sure he was a brave and strong Shepherd, and that I should be proud to be his son. My mother took such wonderful care of me and my brothers. Five pups! My goodness, we were a handful. But she never complained, and she was never cross. Naturally, she always used to call me Lambie-pie. 'Lambie-pie,' she would say, 'don't mind your brothers when they tease you, because you have such a good heart, and I love you.'"

The Bad Hat had a sneaking suspicion that this was going to be a very *long* thank-you speech.

"I know that Lambie-pie is a very common nickname," Duke said.

Really? Since when? The Bad Hat glanced at MacNulty, who shrugged.

"But," Duke went on, "I still always felt special when she called me that. After the nice people rescued us from the puppy mill, and we went to the service place and everything, my family got separated, and I miss them terribly. And so, I want to thank my dear brothers and mother, along with the lovely rescue people, whose names were—" He stopped. "Well, I'm sure they had very *good* names, just like Jan and Tim, who are so kind to us here on the farm."

Jan and Tim. The Bad Hat didn't laugh, because everything Duke said was so clearly genuine and spoken from the heart. But, it was hard to keep a straight face.

"Oh, and the cooking lady!" Duke said. "I can't forget her! I feel so happy every time I see her. And, of course, I want to thank all of the volunteers, even the ones whose names I don't know." Duke frowned. "Which is mostly all of them, I guess. But, still, I love them very much."

"Don't forget to thank the Academy, and your agent," Benjamin said.

Duke nodded. "Yes, of course. I want to thank the Academy of—um, Cats and Dogs, and my agent, who I didn't know I had, but who I'm sure I really appreciate. And I want to thank *every* animal here at our rescue home, especially Florence and Mad Cap and—"

"The orchestra has started playing," Benjamin said, twirling one paw in the air. "You need to wrap it up, so we can go to commercial."

"Okay," Duke said agreeably. "Thank you, thank you,

thank you, everyone! And—I really *like* all of you. I do! And I hope you like me, too. Thank you!"

Now that the speech was finally over, all of the animals in the room applauded.

"All right, then," Florence said, after a moment. "That was a unique diversion. Thank you, Duke."

Duke smiled shyly, and ducked his head.

The Bad Hat looked around the room until he located Jack, who was up on a love seat, with a smug expression.

"Did you have gravy?" he asked.

Jack nodded. "With our suppers. For lunch, we had fresh chicken mixed into our food!"

The Bad Hat *loved* chicken. "Well, I had fresh chicken, too," he said. "In fact, I killed it, and ate it raw, right in the middle of Main Street!"

There was a brief, pensive silence in the room.

"Yuck," Matilda, the Spaniel mix, said. "That must have been messy."

"And I don't think this town has an actual Main Street," Kerry, the sly multicolored cat, said. "So, your story is unconvincing."

Foiled again. "Okay, it was fried chicken," the Bad Hat said. "A drumstick. I found it in a trash can."

"Yummy!" Duke said, and the other dogs nodded happily, while the cats all winced.

He climbed up onto the love seat next to Jack. "You really shouldn't have abandoned me like that today," he said quietly.

"You left *me* last night, during the storm," Jack said. "So, now we're even."

Okay, fair enough.

The Bad Hat was surprised by how glad he was to see everyone—and how happy the rest of them seemed to be to see *him*. Not that he would be giving up his life on the run or anything, but he couldn't remember the last time anyone had acted as though they were pleased to have him around.

"You and Jack were on the news tonight," Cole said, before the dog even had a chance to tell them about any of the impressive experiences he had had so far.

The Bad Hat stopped chewing his kibble. "What do you mean?"

Cole gestured towards Madeline, who was a very large tiger cat. "She saw it on the television in the kitchen, when she was teasing Monica for scraps."

"No. I was helping her cook," Madeline corrected him.

Well, whatever. "Did they report that I was impressing and enthralling the entire town?" the Bad Hat asked. Except that sounded awfully cuddly for a Bad Hat. "Or, I don't know, maybe that I was terrorizing and alarming people? And that all of the villagers now tremble at the very thought of me? And that the police have issued a BOLO?" *Be on the lookout.*

Madeline shook her head. "They said that Jack was saving people. A man who was going to drown, and a baby who was playing in traffic—and I forget what else."

Figures. "That *he* was saving them?" the Bad Hat asked.

Jack looked even more smug. "They said I'm a hero. I'm *sure* to get adopted now."

"A couple of the people said that there was a mysterious black dog nearby, too. They described you as a black Lab with no collar, and asked your owners to come forward, so that you could be reunited with them," Madeline said.

Florence looked grim. "And poor Joan and Thomas rushed right over to the news station, thinking that you were actually there, waiting for them. That's how the reporters made it sound."

How ridiculous. "The guy who drowned said *Jack* pulled him to shore?" the Bad Hat said. "Some tiny little Terrier dragged a *huge* guy out of the water, all by himself?"

Madeline nodded. "They interviewed him, and he said he wasn't sure, but when he opened his eyes, the first thing he saw was a little Yorkie."

Forget ridiculous; that was *annoying*. And maybe even infuriating. The Bad Hat shook his head with disgust. "But, that isn't at all how it happened. Not even close."

"Well, that's the liberal media for you," Benjamin said. "They never get *anything* right."

Seemed that way in this case. "And you're *sure* the townspeople aren't afraid of me?" the dog asked Madeline. "And anxious and intimidated?"

Madeline shook her head again. "No. They want people to Tweet, or post photos online, and that sort of thing, if they catch a glimpse of you."

Well, this was a fine kettle of fish. A total disaster, even. "I may need to relocate," the Bad Hat said. "Because that's not at all what I had in mind."

"You could start doing really destructive and offensive things," MacNulty suggested. "Change your reputation."

160

Good idea! The dog nodded.

"Don't encourage him," Florence said. "And if you leave town, Bad Hat, won't you have to spend a lot of time commuting for your kibble?"

Oh. Maybe. Yeah. Okay, terrible idea! Completely terrible idea.

"Of course," she said casually, "you could just stay here, and then food wouldn't be an issue at all."

Nope. Not a chance. Because, you know, he was wicked smart for a dog. So, the Bad Hat ignored that suggestion completely. "What are we watching tonight?"

"The fourth episode, and maybe the fifth," Florence said.

Yay!

He enjoyed the show, and was even more pleased when the other animals agreed to change genres and watch an old Western, before everyone went to bed. It actually *did* have horses, and a saloon, and duels, and a lone stalwart cowboy named Shane, and a hero-worshipping little boy—and was altogether excellent. Perfect, even. In fact, he would have been happy to watch it over and over again, every single night, for the rest of his life. The movie made him think that maybe he was all wrong about his destiny. Instead of being a ruthless outcast or a regular topic in pop-culture gossip columns, he should be a mysterious cowboy, and protect and oversee the villagers he encountered. An aloof, but benevolent and confident figure to be admired by one and all.

Or, maybe not. It sounded like it would maybe be too much work.

Benjamin and some of the other cats spent about half an hour debating the ambiguity of the movie's ending—a conversation the Bad Hat tuned out, in favor of eating more kibble. But, the sun was going to come up soon, so it was time for the dogs to return to their kennels, and for him to venture forth into the world again.

"I really think you should stay," Florence said. "You can have plenty of excitement here."

Nope. Not up for discussion. He was a wild thing now, who could not survive in the confines of a shelter. The Bad Hat shook his head.

She sighed. "Very well. But, don't go far, and please allow Joan or Thomas to catch at least one glimpse of you, so that they will be less worried. And come back here again tonight, so that you can have a proper meal."

Those all seemed like reasonable requests. "Will do," the Bad Hat promised.

It was nice to have a full stomach, and to have spent a few hours with pleasant comrades. So, the Bad Hat felt rather lighthearted as he dashed across the meadow.

"Shane!" Jack shouted from his outdoor run. "Come back!"

The dog laughed, and almost *did* go back—before he thought better of the idea. Maybe he was watching too much British television, but he didn't want to start, you know, letting *sentiment* cloud his thinking.

"Good-bye, Shane!" Jack shouted.

"See you at midnight!" the Bad Hat yelled back. "Same time, same place!"

His leap over the fence was a little ungainly, but he made it without hurting himself. When he picked himself up from the ground, MacNulty was standing there, looking bored.

"Took you long enough," MacNulty said.

Wait—what? The Bad Hat did a double-take. "Where did you come from?"

"Originally? I'm not sure," MacNulty said. "Somewhere near North Conway."

Correct answer—to the wrong question. The Bad Hat shook his head. "What I meant was, how did you beat me out here? I was running really fast."

"Oh." MacNulty grinned. "Well, I guess I'm pretty fast myself."

Greyhound fast, apparently. "Okay," the Bad Hat said. "But, what are you doing here?"

"Waiting for you," MacNulty said.

Clearly, but—"Why?" the Bad Hat asked.

"Because Florence and Cole put together an assignment wheel, and I'm supposed to be your buddy today," MacNulty said.

The Bad Hat was going to protest, but knew that he would be wasting his breath. "Fine," he said. "But, you have to keep up, and—don't cramp my style."

MacNulty yawned. "Whatever, Hat Guy. Lead on."

The Bad Hat didn't really have an agenda for the day, other than to wreak havoc and frighten the locals—or maybe help them with their many problems, and also to try to forage for some food. Which were grand and ambitious goals, but meant that they would have to ramble aimlessly for a while, and look for trouble. But, first, he and MacNulty went down to the lake and took a relaxing swim, followed by a nap, on a sun-warmed rock by the shoreline.

"This is pretty nice," MacNulty said sleepily. "Wish we had some snacks, though."

The Bad Hat definitely agreed with that—snacks would be excellent, right about now.

After a while, they decided to stretch their legs and explore some more. They were drifting through a neighborhood of small ranch houses, when they came upon a perplexed sheep standing in the middle of the road.

The Bad Hat stopped, not sure what to make of that.

MacNulty gasped. "Is that what I think it is?"

"If you think it's a sheep, yeah," the Bad Hat said.

MacNulty looked happier than any animal he had ever seen before. "Wow! I mean, just—*wow.*"

For a Border Collie, this must have been a dream come true. MacNulty seemed to be too excited to form complete sentences, so the Bad Hat looked at the sheep, while the sheep looked back at them.

"Wow," MacNulty kept muttering every so often. "Just—wow. Wow!"

They stood there, in the road.

Time passed.

"So," the sheep said finally. "Aren't you going to herd me?"

What? "Wasn't planning on it, no," the Bad Hat said.

The sheep looked impatient. "I'm lost, and I have no idea how to get home. You are dogs, and I need for you to herd me, so I can get back there."

Well, she was yapping at the wrong fella. "Ask this guy," the Bad Hat said, nodding towards the starstruck MacNulty. "I'm not the right kind of dog. Dogs like me fetch things, and most of us can swim pretty well, and we like to lie on couches. We don't, you know, work with *livestock*."

The sheep pulled herself up to her full height. "Is that an insult?"

"No, not at all," the Bad Hat said quickly. "I only—all I meant is that I lack the proper skills."

MacNulty snapped out of his daze. "I can do it! I've *always* wanted to herd." He hesitated. "Only, how do I start?"

The sheep rolled her eyes. "It's really not difficult. You just bark, and range back and forth behind me, and steer me in the right direction. You're allowed to nip *near* my hooves, but never actually to touch them, because that would hurt."

The Bad Hat had a feeling that they had picked the wrong road to run down.

"I can do it," MacNulty said confidently. "I'm sure I can. I must have genetic instincts—I just have to figure out how to access them." Then, he frowned. "But, we don't know where you live, so how do we figure out the right direction?"

The sheep shrugged. "Dogs always know. But, hurry up, please, I don't want to miss my lunch."

She was a mite bossy, in the Bad Hat's opinion, but he decided to keep that to himself.

MacNulty moved forward tentatively, and sniffed at the sheep's feet.

"Hey, watch the hooves!" the sheep said.

"I need to get the scent, and then we'll trace your footsteps back," MacNulty said.

"All right, but be careful," the sheep said, eyeing him with deep suspicion.

The Bad Hat was too polite to say so, but for the record, sheep smelled kind of *rank*. He leaned forward to take a few sniffs of his own, in case MacNulty needed backup.

MacNulty closed his eyes, clearly deep in thought,

and then snuffled around the road for a moment.

"Okay, I've got it," he said. "I'm almost *sure* I've got it. Follow me, and you'll be home soon."

The sheep hesitated. "This isn't normally how herding works. I'm supposed to go first, and you guide me."

Everyone was a critic. "Do you want your lunch or not?" the Bad Hat asked.

"Good point," the sheep said. "I'll be right behind you."

The Bad Hat and MacNulty followed the trail, but it was a really *stupid* trail. First, one direction, and then, another. Across some lawns, along a pine-needle path, into a kid's sandbox, down the road, into the woods, back to the street, through someone's garden—the trail was completely illogical.

"Are you sure this is right?" he asked MacNulty quietly. "It doesn't make much sense."

"Shhh," MacNulty said, sounding very anxious. "I'm trying to concentrate."

So, they followed the twisted route a little longer— ending up right back where they started, in the middle of the road. MacNulty growled something unintelligible under his breath, and put his nose to the ground, looking for a different path.

"Where were you *going*?" the Bad Hat asked the sheep, panting. "This is all over the place."

The sheep thought. At length. "Well, first, I was just meandering around, because it was a pretty day. I ate some clover, that had lovely fresh dew on it. And then, I was looking for flowers, but I couldn't find any." She paused. "I really like flowers."

The Bad Hat nodded cooperatively, hoping that she would move things along.

"All types of flowers," the sheep went on. "I'm not very picky. Although daisies are especially nice."

"Unh-hunh," the Bad Hat said.

"Where was I?" the sheep asked.

How was he supposed to know? It was a long and exhausting anecdote. The Bad Hat shrugged, and looked around for MacNulty, who had put his head inside a bush while he tried to find the scent.

"Well, I ran around," the sheep said. "And then, I realized that I was lost, and I panicked, and I ran around some more, in circles. There were a lot of houses. And then, I had to rest, and then I ran some more, and finally, I just stood in the street for a long time."

Not the most interesting story he had ever heard,

that was for sure. "We can follow the trail," the Bad Hat said, leaving the *because dogs are completely awesome* part unspoken, "but it's going to take a while."

Which it did. Following the erratic circles seemed endless, and the sheep slowed things down even more by running off to one side to admire some pink asters. Then, when an increasingly frantic MacNulty ushered her back to the scent trail, she trundled off again, to look at a bed of day lilies.

"Aren't they gorgeous!" she said.

Yep. Terrific. Wonderful. He couldn't be happier. "Unh-hunh," the Bad Hat said.

MacNulty just groaned.

"We passed my farm a little while ago," the sheep said conversationally. "But, this is so nice, finding flowers together. Maybe we'll come across some salvia. Wouldn't that be exciting?"

Was she kidding? The Bad Hat stared at her. "What about your lunch?"

She considered that. "You're right. There's some hay calling my name right about now." She spun around to go in the opposite direction. "Come on, I think it's this way."

The Bad Hat looked at MacNulty, who seemed to be shell-shocked.

"Buck up, man," he said. "We're in the homestretch now. You can do it!"

"Trail," MacNulty said feverishly. "Must follow trail. Must herd."

"That's right," the Bad Hat said. "Keep that laser-like focus. I'm rooting for you, big guy."

MacNulty staggered along the trail, while the sheep prattled happily about goldenrod and black-eyed Susans and forsythia and lupine and all. Finally, they came to a large pasture, which was full of grazing sheep.

"Look," the Bad Hat said. "It's the Border Collie Holy Grail!"

MacNulty just mumbled some more, shaking his head back and forth.

A large ram came thundering over to the fence. "Where have you been, Amaryllis?"

The sheep motioned towards the dogs. "Looking for flowers, with my new friends. We had such a good time!"

The ram frowned at them. "She is not *ever* supposed to leave the pasture. I hold you two accountable for this!"

"It won't happen again, sir," the Bad Hat said. If there was any justice in the world, that is.

"It had better not," the ram said, and then pushed some of the fence wires aside so that Amaryllis could squeeze through the hole and into the pasture.

"Come back soon!" Amaryllis called. "We'll go jaunting again!"

Oh, yeah. Without a doubt. "Good luck with your floriculture," the Bad Hat said, and led the shaky MacNulty away.

If he had to it do over, he probably would have suggested that instead of exploring, they should just spend the entire day napping!

CHAPTER ELEVEN

The Bad Hat waited until they were safely away from the sheep farm, and then sat down in a nice, shady spot under some trees.

"Come on," he said. "Get out of the sun for a minute."

MacNulty nodded, lurched over to some thick grass, and lay down on his side, gasping.

"You all right?" the Bad Hat asked.

MacNulty stared at him with those glassy eyes. "That was *awful*."

By the Bad Hat's standards, it had mostly just been annoying, but okay, whatever.

"My life is meaningless," MacNulty said. "It's all ashes."

Whoa, they were *way* out of his skill set now. The

Bad Hat really wasn't going to be comfortable having a conversation about things like philosophy, and *emotions*. "Well, gosh," he said, for lack of a better idea.

It was quiet, except for the sounds of a tractor somewhere in the distance and the buzzing of unknown insects.

"My whole life," MacNulty said shakily, "my only dream was to be able to herd. Herding was my reason for being. My destiny! Only, I finally got a chance to do it—and it turns out that sheep are *horrible*." He shuddered. "I don't even *like* them."

The Bad Hat was not currently a big fan of sheep, either.

"Now I have to question *everything*," MacNulty said. "Am I real? Do I exist? What if it's all nothingness, and the entire world is a figment of my imagination?"

The Bad Hat couldn't think of a single sensible way to respond to that—so, he didn't say anything at all.

MacNulty dragged himself up off the grass. "I'm going home."

Was he really leaving, or just being dramatic? "We don't *have* a home," the Bad Hat said. "And what about Florence's rule? You're supposed to stay with me."

"Sorry," MacNulty said. "I have to go get some kibble. I need to ground myself."

That sounded like a joke, but apparently, it wasn't, because MacNulty started trudging down the road without ever looking back.

The Bad Hat stood underneath the trees, feeling quite bereft. What was the point of having a buddy system, if they all kept leaving him?

Although it was further proof that most dogs simply weren't cut out to be a Bad Hat. They cracked under the pressure, and wilted like little flowers. *He* was made of sterner stuff than that.

Which didn't mean that he wouldn't mind going home to have some lunch.

But, since he was the Bad Hat and should be above such petty concerns, maybe he would walk around town, instead, and see if there were any new adventures to be had.

He was moseying down a deserted road, when a dark blue pickup truck came careening around a curve. The Bad Hat dodged into the underbrush, wanting to be sure that he would be safely out of the way of such an irresponsible driver. The truck sped past him, raising a thick cloud of dirt, which made him cough.

Then, the truck slowed down slightly, and someone in the passenger's seat tossed a large bag out of the window. It landed by the side of the road, and then the truck swerved away, until it was out of sight.

Weird. And it was also littering. The Bad Hat might be a ruthless rebel, but he did not approve of littering.

Maybe he should drag the bag into the bushes, so that the street would look more tidy. Not that he was running for Good Citizen of the Year, but the black trash bag looked ugly, lying there on the pavement.

He was about to pick up the bag with his teeth, when it *moved.*

Hey, whoa! Of course, he was nearly impossible to frighten or alarm in any way—but he leaped backwards, feeling his heart start pounding. Garbage that wiggled was creepy.

Could the sack be full of rats? Or worse, *snakes?*

Something inside the bag was still squirming around, and he could hear gasping, and mewing, and—mewing?

Cats!

He used his front paws to tear a hole in the bag, and discovered a bunch of kittens—all of whom screamed when they saw him.

"Calm down," the Bad Hat said. "I'm just trying to—"

"Ack!" one of the kittens screeched. Then, it toppled over and lay still.

Was it *dead*? "What's wrong with him?" the dog asked, trying not to panic. "Is he okay?"

"Harold faints sometimes," another kitten said. "Hit him, everyone, until he wakes up!"

To the Bad Hat's appalled amazement, the other kittens all began whacking the unconscious one with their paws.

"No, no, don't do that!" he said. "You'll hurt him. Didn't your mother ever teach any of you how to behave?"

In response, the kittens started crying, and calling for their mother, and just generally going to pieces.

Wow. This was terrible. The Bad Hat bent his head, and cautiously puffed a gentle breath into the unconscious kitten's face.

The kitten woke up, fluttered his eyes, stared at the Bad Hat for a second, then said, "Ack!" and passed out again. In the meantime, the other kittens wailed loudly, without even seeming to pause to breathe.

Since he had no idea what to do, the Bad Hat sat down for a minute and panted as hard as he could.

Okay, he needed to pull himself together. Someone around here had to be calm, and think clearly—and he was pretty sure that none of the kittens were up for the job.

"Kittens, just take it easy," he said. "Tell me where you live, and I'll bring you home to your mother, okay?"

The only response was more hysterical crying.

So, the dog panted for a while longer, and thought about running away, and maybe hiding somewhere for the next week or two.

"Please," he said finally. "Can one of you tell me what happened?"

It took a while, but several of them explained in ear-splitting unison—how many were there, a *hundred?*—that the mean people had taken them away from their mother, because they wanted to get rid of them forever, and that they were scared, and that it had been hard to breathe inside the bag, and that they missed their mother, and they wanted to go home, but they were afraid of the people—and it just went on and on.

"Where do you live?" the Bad Hat asked, once they had finally run out of steam—and things to say.

The kittens all looked at each other, and shrugged. None of them said anything, except for Harold, who woke up briefly, took another look at the dog, said "Ack!" and slumped down again. But, the rest of them were now being less noisy, at least, and the dog took advantage of the relative peace to count them.

Six. Funny, they sounded like an *army* of kittens, but there were only six.

"Tell me about your home," the Bad Hat said. "I need some clues."

They all talked as loudly as they could, trying to shout over each other, which gave him a headache.

"One at a time," the dog said.

They all looked at each other, and then, a little black kitten with white paws spoke up.

"There was grass," she said.

"And a house," a second one added.

"And—maybe a tree," a third one contributed.

The Bad Hat nodded, waiting for more information, but they seemed to be finished. "Is that it? You don't have any details?"

There was another very long pause, as they all thought.

"Dirt, maybe?" one of them said uncertainly.

The others nodded.

"There was dirt," another one agreed. "We lived outside, and it was cold."

The Bad Hat listened patiently, while they all talked about how cold it was, and how scared and sad they were, and how hungry they were—and a whole new round of crying and mewing started.

At some point during all of this, Harold woke up again.

"Where am I?" he asked, and then gasped when he saw the dog. "Ack—"

"Don't!" the Bad Hat ordered. "Stay awake this time!"

"Okay," Harold said obediently, and sat down on his tiny haunches, instead of passing out. "Why are they crying?"

"They're upset," the dog said.

Which was the understatement of the year.

"Oh," Harold looked around, his eyes that sort of milky blue color that very young kittens had. "Where's Mommy? Can we find her?"

"She's gone!" one of his siblings said through stormy tears. "We'll never see her again! We live in a nightmare!"

Harold thought about that, blinked, then said "Ack!" and toppled over again.

Of all the roads, in all the towns, in all the world, these kittens had had to be dumped on the one where *he* was? The Bad Hat panted some more.

"Okay," he said, once that was out of his system. "I know a safe place to take you. Once we get there, my friends—" Oops! "I mean my, uh, *colleagues* will help us figure out what to do next. But, right now, I need for you all to relax, and have, um, Quiet Time."

The kittens promptly closed their mouths, and were silent.

Thank goodness. Now, he could hear himself think. "It's at least a mile away from here. Are you all good at walking?"

They looked at him, their mouths still shut.

"Can you walk that far?" he asked. "Because it would be very helpful if I knew that."

They stared at him with their glistening little eyes. Some of them shuddered and trembled and shook, but none of them made a sound.

Great. Just great. At this point, he felt like lying down and crying, too—for about a month straight.

The Bad Hat took a deep breath. "Please tell me if you can walk, or if we need to make a different plan."

"We're having Quiet Time," one of the kittens whispered.

Oh. Right. Fine. He would simply make an executive decision, then. "I want all of you to climb back into the bag, so I can carry you," he said.

None of them budged.

"Please," he said.

"Can we move during Quiet Time?" the same kitten asked.

"Yes," the Bad Hat said. "But, only to get into the bag. Then, you can sit and think your silent little thoughts, while I bring you to the safe place."

Cautiously, the kittens crept into the bag and crouched against the black plastic, their eyes looking bigger than ever. Well, five of them did, anyway. Harold was still lying on the road in a crumpled heap.

The Bad Hat gently picked him up by the scruff of his neck, and set him inside the bag. Then, he lifted it off the ground, which made the kittens all tumble against each other and start screaming again.

The Bad Hat put the bag down, and frowned at them. "*Shhh*," he said. "It's Quiet Time."

Upon which, they closed their mouths.

He carried the bag a few hundred feet, and was just

starting to relax when Harold woke up and began yelling that he was suffocating, and had claustrophobia, and needed to be let out of the bag *right this very minute*. Which set the rest of the kittens off, and Quiet Time was very definitely no longer in effect.

The Bad Hat was able to lower the bag to the ground without losing his temper or snapping at anyone—and congratulated himself for being the most gloriously saint-like and kindly dog on the entire planet.

"All right," he said through his teeth. "Everybody, get out of the bag. Then, line up behind me, so that we can walk together. No straggling!"

The kittens weren't very coordinated, but they managed to scramble over each other and out onto the street. They milled around in confusion, and finally lined up, most of them facing in different directions.

"Everyone, face forward," the Bad Hat said.

The kittens maybe didn't understand what "forward" meant, because they all turned around a few times—but, ended up pointing in completely different directions again.

Well, maybe they would catch on, once he started walking.

"Follow me," he said.

The kittens did fairly well for about fifty feet, and

then they started to get bored and cranky, and began scuffling with each other.

"Maybe you could sing," the Bad Hat suggested. "Do you know any songs?"

The kittens shook their heads.

Which would not be a problem if he had a guitar, and they were in the Alps—but, he didn't, and they weren't.

"Can you count?" he asked.

"To three!" one of the kittens said proudly.

The Bad Hat nodded. "That's very good. So, you can count our steps, while we walk."

They made it another fifty feet or so, with the kittens shouting, "One! Two! Three!" over and over. Then, the chant petered out, as they got tired, and started stumbling and wandering all over the road.

He was beginning to understand why people made jokes about the notion of herding cats. Sheep might be challenging, but poor MacNulty would be stymied—and distressed—even more by *this* group.

So, the Bad Hat lay down by the side of the road, and took slow, deep breaths to try and collect himself.

"Oh, no, he fainted!" one of the kittens yelled, and they all ran over and started swatting him.

Two kittens even climbed up on his back, and smacked his ears violently with their paws.

The Bad Hat was going to yell at them, but then, he thought of a possible solution to this mess.

"Everyone else, climb up on me, too," he said. "I'll carry you piggyback."

"But, I thought you were a dog," one of the kittens protested. "You are weird-looking, if you're a pig."

Grrr. And double-*grrr.* "This isn't a species thing," the Bad Hat said. "The point is that I'm going to give you a ride to the nice rescue group, and we will all be very, *very* happy, and act like little angels, and then have some tasty and nutritious food. *Got it?*"

All of the kittens climbed meekly up onto his back—except for Harold, who stayed on the pavement.

"Is there a problem?" the Bad Hat asked.

Harold nodded. "I'm afraid of heights," he said, in a voice so small that the dog had to lean closer to hear him.

Naturally. "Then, you will have to keep your eyes closed," the Bad Hat said. "Mount up, soldier!"

Harold shrugged, and climbed onto his back.

Once he was sure the kittens were all perched there,

the Bad Hat stood up very slowly, while they clung to him and shrieked a few times.

"Hang on tightly, close your eyes, and have Quiet Time until I tell you to stop," the Bad Hat said.

Then, he started down the street, with the kittens gripping his fur precariously and squeaking now and again. But, other than that, they behaved. Mostly.

If anyone saw him like this, covered with weepy kittens, he would *never* live it down.

CHAPTER TWELVE

Every so often, one of the kittens would fall off, and the Bad Hat would have to stop, crouch down, and wait for it to climb back on. He tried to stay on back roads as much as possible, to keep out of sight. But, when he passed a small farm stand, which was selling fresh produce, people laughed and pointed and took pictures of them with their cell phones.

The Bad Hat just plodded grimly on. It was going to be a problem if anyone chased him, because he wasn't sure he could run, without ending up with kittens strewn all over the road.

But, people only seemed to be interested in chuckling and taking photographs or videos of a large black dog with six vocal kittens riding and swaying on his back.

He made steady progress towards the rescue group's farm, although here and there, one of the kittens would topple off his back again, land on the ground, and cry. So, he would have to comfort the kitten, and then somehow convince it to get up there again. And again. And *again.*

This was not a speedy or efficient process.

It was a huge relief when he finally glimpsed the meadow in the distance.

"Cheer up," he said, since some of the kittens were wailing again, because even riding on his back was tiring them out. "We're almost there."

He certainly couldn't blame them for crying, because if he were a baby kitten who had been snatched away from his mother and thrown away in a bag like yesterday's trash, he would be crying his eyes out, too. So, their small exhausted sobs seemed pretty rational, under the circumstances.

Most of the dogs were out in the meadow, running and chasing each other, and as he approached, they gathered by the fence to stare at him.

"I have never seen anything more horrifying in my life," MacNulty said. "And I've been *around.*"

Lancelot nodded. "It's humiliating, dude. You're, like, a disgrace to every other dog in the world."

Yeah, yeah, he knew that already. The Bad Hat sighed.

"Hooray, you brought us kittens for lunch!" Jack shouted, and laughed so hard that he actually fell down.

The kittens all screamed in terror, and dug into the Bad Hat's back with their little needle claws. Then, he heard an "Ack!" and felt a small thump by his neck.

"Oh, that's not good," MacNulty said. "That's not good at all. One of them just up and died."

"What?" Jack jumped to his feet. "But, I was kidding. I don't want to eat them. Why did it die?"

"You scared it to death," Duke said, his eyes huge. "Oh my goodness, this is terrible! What are we going to do? Does anyone know cat CPR?"

The Bad Hat shook his head. "No, that's just Harold. He's prone to fainting spells. I think he has anxiety issues."

Matilda, the small Spaniel mix, frowned through the fence. "I don't know, Bad Hat. He looks pretty dead to me."

Inside the house, the cats must have heard the kittens screaming bloody murder, because when the Bad Hat looked over there, he could see angry little feline eyes glaring at him from almost every single window.

"Just help me out, guys," the Bad Hat said. "Please? I don't know what to do next."

"Learn to juggle?" MacNulty suggested.

"Become a stay-at-home dad?" Rachel contributed.

"Never show your face in public again?" Lancelot said.

Three pretty good ideas.

"Drop 'em off up at the front door, and then run like crazy," Natasha, a Beagle Terrier mix he didn't know very well, said.

Oh, they had a winner! The Bad Hat nodded. "That's perfect, yeah. Thanks."

He brought the kittens up to the porch, and then crouched down so that they could slide off him to safety. At least one of them yelled, "Whee!" so they must have enjoyed the trip. Then, he barked twice.

No answer.

So, he barked a few more times, until the door opened.

"Webster!" Joan said, sounding surprised—and delighted. "I'm so glad to see you. And—you've brought guests?" She swung the door open wider. "Won't you come in?"

Her voice was so casual, that the Bad Hat almost fell

for that and stepped inside. Instead, he lowered his fore-legs and gave his back a quick twitch, so that the still-unconscious Harold would land gently on the doormat.

"Oh, the poor little thing," Joan said, and scooped Harold up. "Thank you, Webster."

It was a relief to see Florence's shaky head peeking out from behind her.

"I found them a little while ago," he barked at her. "Some idiots put them in a bag and then threw it out of a truck."

Florence shook her head, and came stumping out to the doormat, making nurturing sounds.

The kittens immediately flung themselves on her, all of them chattering at once. Naturally, they knocked her down, but she found her way back to her feet and began to usher them inside the house.

Joan reached out her free hand. "Come on, Webster," she said. "How about some lunch?"

So tempting. Almost irresistible, even.

He knew she was going to make a move to catch him— which she did—but, she was easy enough to avoid. He was pleasant about it, though, and tried to make it seem playful.

Then, he barked once, and galloped away. He did

pause long enough to yell "See ya tonight!" at the dogs in the meadow, and then headed straight for the woods.

It had been a pretty stressful morning. Lunch would have been nice.

And he wasn't at all tempted to give up, go back to the rescue farm, and lead a more predictable life from now on.

Nope. Not the Baddest of Bad Hats.

And it wasn't like he didn't have a million better things to do. The fact that he couldn't think of any of them at the moment wasn't important.

But, he was surprised to find himself feeling mopey as he walked around town. It was almost as though he *liked* having friends, and being part of something. And he certainly liked having lunch. Right now, he was even homesick for the sound "Ack!" and the reliable thud that always followed it.

A few of the people he passed seemed to recognize him, and some of them called him by name, took his photo, tried to catch him—or all three. Was he really becoming a media sensation? Seemed that way. But, it didn't feel as appealing as the idea had seemed a few days ago. Canine icons apparently had a pretty lonely time. So, he avoided the attention as much as possible, and tried to maintain a low profile.

He knew he should probably keep to himself for the rest of the day, since people seemed to be so determined to rescue him. But, he went to the village green, because the food in the trash cans behind the restaurant was bound to be delicious, and he hadn't eaten for hours.

He hid in the bandstand for a while, to make sure the coast was clear. Then, he took a deep breath and dashed towards the restaurant.

"Look, it's that dog!" someone shouted, from the steps of the general store. "The one from the Internet!"

Fame was a heavy burden. The Bad Hat tried to carry it gracefully, though. But, the sad truth was that he had been recognized, and the cell phone cameras were popping out all over the place.

Being a celebrity simply was not all that it was cracked up to be.

There was a great flurry of excitement, and people came rushing out of the post office and the restaurant to catch a glimpse of him. One of the diners was so excited, that he actually started choking on the sandwich he was eating.

Nobody noticed at first, and then someone tried to perform the Heimlich maneuver on him, but didn't do the technique correctly.

The Bad Hat changed directions, and raced directly towards the choking man. He hit him at top-speed, with a deft head-butt to the diaphragm, including the proper upward push. The food the man had been choking on immediately flew out of his mouth, and he started gasping for breath.

"Oh, thank you," he said weakly. "Thank you so much."

The dog waited long enough to make sure that the guy really was okay, grabbed half of an uneaten grilled cheese sandwich from the nearest plate, and then bolted back across the village green, and away. Speed of lightning, roar of thunder—that was him, all right.

Since his celebrity status was growing much faster than he had expected, it seemed as though the safest thing to do was just to nap quietly, until it was time for the viewing party. He had to estimate when it was around midnight, by looking up at the moon—not that he knew much of anything about stars or the solar system or planets. But, he took an educated guess, and then headed towards Green Meadows Rescue Group's Farm.

The house was dark, except for a low light up in Joan and Thomas's room. Maybe they were up reading? Still, he waited for a while, to see if it would go out. Unfortunately, it didn't. He passed a few minutes with the owl, who was eating a chestnut—and very cranky about the taste of tannic acid. But, at least the owl got a good yuk out of it, when the dog tried to leap over the fence in one great bound, and fell over the top into the mud.

"Oh, that's one for the ages," the owl said, chuckling. "Wish I had a video camera."

"I did it on purpose," the Bad Hat said. "To give you a laugh."

"Okay. Keep telling yourself that," the owl said, chuckling harder.

The door, once again, had been left open, and this time, Jack was the one waiting for him.

"Hey best friend," he said, happily. "You're famous. You even have your own Facebook page!"

Seriously? That was kind of cool. "Does it have a lot of fans?" the Bad Hat asked.

Jack nodded. "Pretty much the whole town, and now other people from all over the place are clicking on it, too. It's called Wandering Webster, and talks about you being a lost dog who needs help and everything."

Yuck.

"I know," Jack said, reading his expression. "Everyone's in the den right now, making fun of you about it."

No doubt.

"Here's our Little Wanderer," MacNulty said when he and Jack walked into the room, and the rest of the animals cracked up completely.

Okay, he had to remember that he was awfully suave. He could rise above this. "You all just wish *you* had a Facebook page and were worshipped by the masses," the Bad Hat said. "Besides, *buddy*, you left me out there all alone today, and I ended up having to deal with a thousand neurotic kittens by myself. Turncoat!"

"Cat lover!" MacNulty said, without missing a beat.

"Sheep hater!" the Bad Hat said.

MacNulty nodded glumly. "Cat lover," he said, under his breath.

Yeah. So? "Sorry about the sheep, and you no longer having a reason to live," the Bad Hat said.

"I know," MacNulty said, looking unhappy. Then, his expression brightened. "Hey, wait a minute. Cows!"

What? The dog looked at him curiously.

"I'm going to get adopted, and then herd *cows*," MacNulty said. "I bet cows are *wonderful!*"

Well—maybe. But, it was nice that he had a new goal in life. The Bad Hat turned to look at everyone else. "Anyway. What are we watching tonight?"

Benjamin snickered. "You really think it's going to be that easy? We're planning to make fun of you for at least another hour."

Which he quite possibly deserved. "How are the kittens?" he asked.

Pico let out a sigh. "Making a terrible ruckus. I couldn't get any sleep at all up there. Joan and Thomas are taking turns feeding them with baby bottles."

"Well, they like to make noise, that's for sure," the Bad Hat said, settling down on a couch and getting ready to stuff himself with kibble. He was *starving.* "Are they all okay? Especially Harold?"

"Ack!" Pico said, and pretended to faint.

That must have meant that they were all right, but that it was business as usual for poor Harold.

"They're devastated about their mother," Florence said. "So, it's hard to keep them calm. But, Dr. K. was over here this afternoon, and they all checked out fine, even the wobbly one."

All of the animals nodded solemnly. People didn't always realize that one thing most stray animals had in common was that they missed their mothers terribly. A lucky few had known their fathers, and some strays knew that their mothers had been safely adopted, and could relax about that. Once in a while, the Bad Hat had even heard of puppies and kittens who had gotten adopted along *with* their mothers, and got to stay with them always. But, that almost never happened.

The room was very quiet, and he suspected that everyone was feeling as mournful as he was right now, as they remembered their families.

Duke was the first one to speak. "My mother and two of my brothers are service dogs," he said proudly. "After the puppy mill, we all went to the service place for training, and they were stars! But, my brother Rex—oh, he was such a scamp!—was maybe too fierce, and for me, the tricks they wanted us to do were very, very hard. My mother said, 'Lambie-pie, don't you worry about a thing. You are so special, and I know you will find your place in the world.' There was so much sadness in my heart when

I had to get on the big truck and leave. I'll never forget that." He paused, lowering his head for a moment.

The rest of the animals did the same, out of respect.

"So," Duke continued, "Rex and I went to the K-9 Training Academy, and he did such a wonderful job! But, I wasn't very good at climbing all of the tall walls and the ladders, and I certainly did not *ever* want to bite the man in the puffy suit. So, I ended up here, but I do hope that I get to see my loved ones again someday. They are all so successful! I'm really proud of them!"

Duke was so genuinely good that the Bad Hat couldn't help finding it charming.

"But, when I get adopted," Duke said, "I hope my new family finds some jobs for me to do sometimes. I would like to be able to work."

"Me, too," MacNulty said enthusiastically. "This couple adopted me from the shelter in Concord, but they brought me back because I was 'too energetic.' What does that even mean?"

Other animals chimed in with the arbitrary and shallow reasons they had been rejected by owners—too big, too small, barked too often, meowed too loudly, ate too much, scratched the couch, had an accident on the rug, tipped over the trash can, climbed the curtains, were the "wrong" color, got on the bed, and other pretty minor complaints. And, of course, lots of people who adopted pets suddenly decided that they were allergic to them— and immediately got rid of the animals. As far as the Bad Hat was concerned, they should have figured out whether they were allergic *before* they broke some poor dog's or cat's heart.

"I *did* bite some people," Matthew, the feral cat, admitted. "All the time. I should probably stop doing that."

Well, yeah. Maybe that particular complaint had been reasonable.

A lot of the animals didn't want to talk about their families, or how they had ended up at the shelter, the Bad Hat noticed. But, as far as he could tell, most of the animals' memories were similar stories. Being cold and hungry and frightened, and being taken away from their families. After a while, the emotions in the room were running pretty high, and more than a few of them were sniffling.

"You always make jokes about the rest of us," Kerry said to Benjamin, "but you never talk about what it was like when *you* were a kitten."

"Mother was a Chocolate Point," Benjamin said, and—to the Bad Hat's shock—the cat was completely overcome, and began to weep without giving any further details. He was discreet about it, but seemed to be inconsolable, even when Kerry patted him on the head with her paw.

Wow. Maybe that was the thing they all had in common in the rescue group, no matter how different they were— they all had unhappy pasts, and upsetting memories.

By this point, enough animals in the room were crying, so that the Bad Hat was pretty sure that they might need to watch *E.T.* again tonight, to get the misery out of their systems. He glanced at Florence, whose little crossed eyes were staring off into the distance, so she must have been revisiting old, difficult memories, too.

"Well, I'll tell you what," Jack said, breaking the relative silence. "My mother was *scrappy*. She had something to say about everything, and wow, she made sure that no one messed with us!" He paused. "I think some nice rich people adopted her, and she lives in Boston in a big mansion, with servants to feed and bathe her, and give her as many treats as she wants, whenever she wants."

The Bad Hat glanced at Florence, who was now

looking at Jack so compassionately, that he suspected that the real story of Jack's family didn't have such a happy ending.

"I bet she wears ribbons every day," the Bad Hat said, trying to keep the mood in the room light, "and two on Sundays."

Jack laughed. "Of course she does, and looks just as pretty as can be. Imagine how terrible *you* would look in a ribbon? They would have to tape it to your silly shiny head."

The Bad Hat was pretty proud of how sleek his fur was, although he wasn't about to admit it. And, of course, he wasn't what you'd call a Ribbon Guy.

Benjamin had been busy washing his face, pretending that he had not cried at all, but now, he cleared his throat. "Enough with the nostalgia already. Let's watch *It's a Wonderful Life.*"

There was general agreement about this, and the Bad Hat settled back to enjoy the show. And—just like always—they laughed, and they cried, and they were on the edge of their seats. In fact, they liked it so much that they watched it twice. Jimmy Stewart, the star, was maybe even more cool than Alan Ladd in *Shane*. The

Bad Hat would have to find out if Jimmy Stewart had ever been in a cowboy movie, because that would be really fun to see.

As dawn approached, he was surprised to feel a sense of *dread* about having to leave. Maybe he, um, wanted to *stay* here? And let his colleagues be his *friends*, once and for all, and—

"Bad Hat, I need to talk to you," Florence said quietly.

Good. He would pretend he wanted to go off into the big, scary world, but then let her talk him into changing his mind, and that would preserve his dignity.

"Come on," she said, and walked him to the door.

So, maybe she was going to make a last-minute effort to get him to stay? Unless she *wanted* him to leave? Maybe that was it. He followed her, feeling his tail droop a little.

"Um, look. I kind of, maybe—" he started. "I mean, I'm not sure if—"

"You have an important job today, Bad Hat," she said.

What? He cocked his head. Did she want him to do *chores*, or something?

"You need to find their mother," Florence said, looking very serious. "Owners who would simply discard kittens that way won't be taking good care of their mother, either. I'm very concerned that she's in danger, so you need to bring her here, where we can take care of her."

Oh. Okay. Looked like he wasn't going to be staying, after all. "I think you're probably right," he said, "but how am I going to do that? When I asked the kittens where they lived, all they could tell me was that there was a house, with some grass, and that there might be a tree." Dirt, also.

Which was sort of *beyond* vague.

"You'll find her," Florence said. "I have great faith in you."

The Bad Hat blinked, caught off guard by that. "You do?"

Florence nodded. "Yes, I most certainly do. I wasn't really sure about you, at first, but you have become a wonderful friend, and a credit to all of us. I'm so very fond of you."

Hearing that, the Bad Hat actually felt tears in his eyes. "Really?" he said. "No one has ever been fond of me before."

Florence reached a shaky paw out, and touched his front leg for a moment. "Oh, I think your mother was *extremely* fond of you. You are a very good dog, in spite of your best efforts."

He hoped so. He hoped so very much. He had to blink some more, fighting the tears, all sorts of unexpected emotions welling up in his heart.

"There's a lot of ground to cover, so I've put together a team, to work with you," she said. "All of the dogs volunteered, but I assigned the ones who will be the most helpful." Florence paused. "And Jack's coming, too."

A team. He had never been part of a *team* before.

"You can do it," she said. "I'll see you back here soon."

The Bad Hat nodded without another word, and trotted outside. It took him three tries to make it over the tall fence. When he finally landed on the other side, Jack, MacNulty, Matilda, Duke, Lancelot, and Rachel were all waiting for him.

"How did you guys make it out here so quickly?" he asked, as he picked himself up. Especially Jack. How on earth could he scramble over such a high fence?

The other dogs exchanged glances, and snickered.

"We're magic, dude," Lancelot drawled. "Pure magic."

The other dogs all nodded, and laughed again.

Clearly, the Bad Had was missing something here. "Seriously. How did you get out here so fast?"

Jack laughed some more. "You are such a bozo. We have a *tun*—"

"Shhh!" MacNulty said.

"—*nel*," Jack finished more softly.

The Bad Hat was still lost. Tun? Nel? What were a "tun" and—wait, he meant a *tunnel*. A tunnel! Well, okay, that would explain everything. "Where is it?" he asked.

Jack started to say something, but MacNulty promptly head-butted him to the ground.

"I don't think we should be wasting time," Rachel said mildly. "The mother cat needs our help."

Right. They needed to focus. "Okay, fine. I know this is a team," the Bad Hat said, "but Florence put me in charge. So, that makes me the captain."

"Then, I'm a colonel," Jack said. "You can call me Colonel Jack."

"And I'm a brigadier general," Matilda, the Spaniel mix, said.

"Since I'm a police dog, I must be a *chief*," Duke said.

MacNulty decided that he was a major general, Lancelot proclaimed that he was a rear admiral, and Rachel dubbed herself a lieutenant general.

The Bad Hat had only seen a couple of war movies, so he had to think for a minute, to digest all of those ranks. "Wait, does that mean that I'm suddenly the lowest-ranking officer here?" he asked.

The other dogs nodded.

"If you do well," Duke said kindly, "you can work your way up to major."

What exciting news.

"What's the plan?" Jack asked, bouncing up and down with excitement. "It's so cool to be part of a rescue mission!"

Everyone looked at the Bad Hat.

Ah, so he had a lower rank, but was apparently still in charge. "The kittens didn't have much information," he said. "They told me that there was grass, and a house, and some dirt, and maybe a tree. They didn't say any-thing about the lake, so the house probably isn't right on the water."

The other dogs waited expectantly for more infor-mation.

"Sorry," the Bad Hat said. "That's all I have."

"So, I guess we probably need to check every single house in town," MacNulty said. "Eventually, we'll find the right one."

The Bad Hat nodded. It wasn't a *great* plan, but at least, it was a plan.

And he was absolutely *determined* that they were going to find the mother cat!

CHAPTER THIRTEEN

So, they started searching. The town might not have been huge, but it covered a pretty wide area. It occurred to the Bad Hat that the cruel owners of the mother cat might not even *live* in this town—they could have driven over from some other village.

Which he decided not to mention just yet, since it was a little demoralizing to think that they could end up walking all over the entire state of New Hampshire for *weeks*, and never find her.

He also didn't make any jokes about looking for a needle in a haystack, because almost every farm they passed actually *had* at least one haystack.

Did cats like hay? Probably not. But, if the mother cat

was scared, and hiding, she could be almost anywhere.

They could rule out any house with no trees in the yard—but so far, they hadn't come across a single house like that.

After searching for a couple of hours with no luck at all, the dogs decided to stop and rest. Rachel found a small wooded clearing, with cool green moss on the ground, and they all flopped down on their sides and panted.

"We're never going to find her," Matilda said. "This is a waste of time."

Probably, but they still had to try. And the stupid truck really *could* have been from anywhere, so they might have to—the Bad Hat lifted his head up from the moss.

"Wait a minute, hold the phone," he said. "We don't have to find the house. We have to find the *truck*."

"And you got a good look at the truck, right, dude?" Lancelot asked.

Well, he'd been diving into the bushes to get out of the way, so it had been more of a *glimpse*—but, that was close enough.

"What do you remember?" Matilda asked eagerly.

"Let's hypnotize him!" Jack said, and snatched a stick

from the ground. Then, he stood right front of the Bad Hat and swung his head back and forth. "Just follow the stick with your eyes, Bad Hat. You are getting very, very *sleepy*."

He *was* kind of sleepy, but it had nothing to do with the silly stick. The Bad Hat yawned. "Give me a break, little man. I'm trying to think."

"But, it's working," Jack said. "You're nodding off."

"I'm *tired*," the Bad Hat said. "So, please don't make me *more* tired."

Jack shrugged, plopped down on the moss, and began to chew the stick.

The Bad Hat closed his eyes, so he could concentrate. Then, he took a few deep breaths, hoping that the refreshing smell of pine trees would clear his mind.

"It was navy blue," he said. "Not new, but not ancient, either. Just, you know, a regular truck. And there was a lot of dried mud and dust and all on the sides, and on the wheels, like they never bothered washing it."

"Someone needs to take mental notes," Rachel said. "Can anyone take notes?"

"I will," MacNulty said. "I have a very good memory." He winced. "But, remind me to erase *sheep* from it, okay?"

The Bad Hat closed his eyes more tightly, trying to bring up a clear image of the speeding truck in his mind. "There was a dent," he said. "On the back right bumper. And—" Was there anything else? Anything at all? He thought as hard as he could, and remembered— flapping. What could have been *flapping*? He opened his eyes. "Rope! There was like, a light blue covering over the truck bed, and it was tied down with old yellow rope. That awful plastic kind, that hurts your teeth."

All of the other dogs shuddered.

"But, it wasn't tied very well, so it was blowing around in the wind," the Bad Hat said. He thought some more and shook his head. "That's it. I don't remember anything else."

"Actually, that's really good," Matilda said. "We can narrow things down a lot that way."

Duke nodded. "Nice police work, Mad Cap. You'll make detective one of these days!"

That didn't sound very enticing, so the dog just shrugged.

They decided to start from the road where he had found the bag of kittens. Then, they could work their way out from there.

The Bad Hat figured that people who threw kittens away couldn't be very smart—and were obviously too lazy to try and do the right thing, and at least drop them off at an animal shelter or the police station or something. So, they were probably also not ambitious enough to drive *miles* out of their way to commit their rat-fink form of animal abuse.

His best guess was that the people had driven to the nearest deserted road, just far enough away from their house, so that if anyone found the kittens, they couldn't be traced back to them. It was a crime of opportunity— not, like, a crime of *intellect*.

They made their search as methodical and logical as possible. Up one street, down the next, checking each side street and all of the little dead-end roads that seemed to appear in the most unexpected wooded spots. They checked garages, too, in case the bad people had parked their truck inside. Then, once they had completely explored an area, they would move one street over and start the process all over again.

Every so often, the Bad Hat would see a truck parked in a driveway or something, and get excited, but it would turn out to be black, or dark green, or too new, or too old, or some other disqualifying factor.

A couple of times, they even came across trucks with dented bumpers, and the Bad Hat would go over and study the vehicle carefully, but it was never the right one.

After a while, they had looked at so many houses and barns and other properties, that the buildings were all starting to blur together. The Bad Hat started worrying that maybe they had *already* passed the right house, and the people just hadn't been home, so the truck wasn't there.

Which meant that they might have to do all of this *again* later.

"Gotta rest," Lancelot said, at one point, breathing hard.

Everyone was worn out, even Rachel and her long Greyhound legs, so they all dropped in their tracks. The Bad Hat didn't even notice that he had landed right in the middle of a mud puddle—until he had already gotten wet. But, he was too tired to move, so he just stayed there and panted for a while.

Finally, they dragged themselves to their feet, and resumed the search. Up streets, down streets, around corners, and then, on to the next section of town. Pickup trucks, full-size vans, minivans, SUVs, small wagons, hybrids, motorcycles, bicycles, skateboards, tractors—lots of forms of transportation, in lots of different driveways.

Many of the houses and cottages were clearly closed up for the season, but they were careful, and checked them, too. Just in case.

The sun was beating down, and it felt very hot. The Bad Hat was hungry, of course—because he was *always* hungry—but, he was also thirsty, and the water in mud puddles tasted terrible. Maybe they should take a detour over to the lake, and drink from it? But, he was too tuckered out even to make the suggestion to the others.

They turned down yet another street. More houses. Big houses. Small houses. Ramshackle houses, which looked more like—

"Hey!" MacNulty said suddenly. "Check it out!"

Just up the road, there was a beat-up old house, with tilted shingles, and an unmown lawn. But, parked in the rutted dirt driveway was a navy-blue truck, with a dented fender, a hanging piece of yellow rope, and a blue tarpaulin draped over the back.

"Wow, my hypnosis was *excellent*," Jack said. "Look how well I made you remember, Bad Hat!"

It was because of dumb luck, not hypnosis, but yes! They had found the house!

The Bad Hat wanted to run down the driveway, barking his head off, but he held back for a second to think.

"Let's charge the house!" Jack said.

Which sounded like a good idea to the Bad Hat, too. But, if bad, thoughtless people lived here, it might make more sense to be sneaky.

"We should take it a little slow," the Bad Hat said. "Get a feel for things, first."

"Reconnaissance!" MacNulty said happily.

Yes, they should do recon first. And it was such a totally cool word, too. The Bad Hat nodded, and followed the others as they retreated into the bushes and observed the house for a while.

There were no signs of activity, although they could hear a television blaring inside somewhere. The house needed a fresh coat of paint, and none of the windows had curtains, although a few had broken shades, all of which were pulled down most of the way. One of the windows was broken, and had been patched with some duct tape and a piece of cardboard.

There was a mildewed old woodpile next to one side of the house, and what looked like a propane gas tank on the other side. There was a weather-beaten porch in the front, with a missing step, and some crooked wooden lattice pieces propped up along the bottom.

The Bad Hat was going to sniff the air, carefully, to catch a whiff of cat or kitten—but, before he could, he heard the sound of a cat crying miserably to herself, from—where?

"I hear a cat," he said. "Does anyone else hear a cat?"

They all listened intently, with their noses pointed in the air, in case they could pinpoint the scent, too.

They listened, until they located the sound under the porch.

What an awful thing to hear. She sounded so desolate.

"Since I'm the captain, I'll go up ahead, and check things out," the Bad Hat said, and the others nodded.

"Don't get caught!" Rachel warned him.

Which would *never* happen, of course. The Bad Hat crept out from the bushes, and made his way slowly across the unkempt yard, to the porch. He poked his head through one of the openings in the boards and was greeted by a loud hiss.

"Get away from me!" the animal said.

It took a moment for the Bad Hat's eyes to adjust to the dim light, but then he saw a black-and-white cat, who had obviously given birth recently, lying on her side in the dirt.

"Hello," he said, with a big smile. "We came to rescue you!"

With an effort, she turned away from him. "Leave me alone," she said, still crying. "I don't *want* to be rescued."

Wait, that wasn't part of the program. Maybe she was kidding. "What?" the Bad Hat said. "But—I mean, we looked for you for *hours.*"

"So?" She slumped down into the dirt. "Go away."

Okay, she had thrown him a real curveball here. The Bad Hat sat and panted for a few seconds. There was probably like, clever psychology he should be using right now, but he didn't know any.

"Are they feeding you?" he asked. "And giving you fresh water? And a soft place to sleep?"

The cat shrugged without lifting her head from the ground. "I don't care what happens to me."

Should he maybe run back to the bushes, and ask the others for advice? Surely, one of them would know what to do. But, he didn't want to risk alerting anyone inside by making any unnecessary noise. "Are, um, the people here nice to you?" he asked. "Is that why you want to stay?"

"No," she said vehemently. "I *hate* it here. But, I'll never leave. I have to stay right in this spot, in case my babies come back."

Whew. That meant that this wasn't possibly beyond him, and he could actually fix this. "Any chance you have, say, six babies?" he asked.

The cat raised her head slightly.

Score! "Including one named Harold?" he asked. "Who faints a lot?"

The cat burst into the hardest animal tears he had ever seen—or heard, and he had certainly been around a lot of animal tears. "My sweet delicate little Harold!" she said. "And Joyce, and Kermit, and Lola, and Mavis, and Ivan! Have you seen them? Are they all right? Do you know where they are?"

As Duke would say, wow, what a lot of questions, and what a lot of names to remember. The Bad Hat nodded. "I found them yesterday, when those creeps"—he motioned towards the house with his head—"threw the bag into the road. And I brought them all to the Green Meadows Rescue Farm. So, they're safe now."

The cat looked at him tremulously. "But—they weren't fully weaned yet. Are you sure they're okay?"

"Yep," he said. "The vet came over and checked them yesterday afternoon, and the people who run the place stayed up all night, feeding them out of baby bottles and keeping them warm on heating pads and all."

Now, the cat looked stunned. "I don't understand. You mean, there are *good* people in the world?"

Amazingly enough, the answer seemed to be yes. He'd met quite a few of them recently. "Yep," he said. "And I'm going to bring you there, too."

The cat started crying again, and he stood there awkwardly, waiting for the gushing tears to pass.

"Is it okay if my friends come out of the woods, so we can figure out the best way to do this?" he asked.

The cat nodded, still weeping.

Whew. He would feel a lot better with some—well—*buddies* to help out. He turned towards the bushes.

"Come on!" he called softly.

The other dogs—his *team*—burst out of the under-brush and raced across the lawn, and watching them made the Bad Hat feel proud. MacNulty and Rachel were in the lead, with Lancelot and Matilda right behind them, while Duke strode in his dignified way through the weeds, and Jack chased after everyone, trying to keep up.

The cat cringed slightly. "That's a lot of dogs," she whispered.

"It's okay," the Bad Hat said. "They're my friends, and you're going to like them."

The dogs gathered in a semicircle around the porch, and everyone barked at once, asking questions and toss-ing out ideas.

"Cool it," the Bad Hat said in a low voice. "That tele-vision in there isn't *that* loud."

The other dogs simmered down a little, but they were still all excited, and anxious, and bumping into each other.

"What do we do?" MacNulty asked. "Do we herd her?"

"I don't think I can walk," the cat said weakly. "I hav-en't had any food for a while, and it's hard to stand up."

The Bad Hat shouldn't have been shocked that people who would discard kittens wouldn't feed their poor mother—even though she was presumably their pet.

"Can you ride on my back?" he asked. "That's how I carried the kittens."

She shook her head. "I don't think I'm strong enough to hang on."

And she was kind of heavy and unwieldy, too, so it would be hard for him to balance her up there. But, they had to do *something*.

"What do we do, if she can't walk, and we can't carry her?" he asked the other dogs.

They all looked at each other, and shrugged, and started panting nervously.

The Bad Hat sat down, and panted, too.

And panted some more.

"We need a branch," Matilda said. "We could use it to drag her. Come on!"

The dogs followed her across the street, and into a small vacant lot, which was covered with trees and bushes and lots of weeds and tall grass.

"It needs to have leaves," Matilda said. "Or a lot of smaller branches. So, she can lie down on it."

"A pine tree!" Rachel said. "That'll be perfect!"

They prowled around the lot until they found a pine tree with branches that were low enough for most of them to reach. The Bad Hat tried to tear one off with his teeth, but the wood was too thick. So, he started chewing the wood, even though the sap was sticky and tasted awful. But, it was taking a long time, and he got impatient.

"This isn't working," he said. "Let's find a different tree."

"No, just break it off," Jack said. "Like this!" He hopped up onto the end of the branch and began jumping up and down. Unfortunately, he was so small that the branch boomeranged back at him and sent him flying through the air. "Oof!" he grunted, when he landed on the ground.

"Pipsqueak's right, though," MacNulty said. "Bad Hat, you and Duke are the biggest—so, you jump on it, until it breaks."

Duke looked at them all blankly. "I don't understand."

"It's okay," the Bad Hat said. "Just do what I do."

The Bad Hat started jumping on the branch, putting all of his weight on his front paws, and Duke cautiously did the same. It took several tries, but finally they pried it off the tree.

"All right!" the Bad Hat said.

"All right!" Duke said, less certainly.

The Bad Hat grabbed the long end in his teeth, and dragged the branch across the street and over to the porch. The other dogs followed him, yapping happily to each other about how *totally awesome* this idea was.

But, when they got to the porch, the cat frowned. "That looks like a *dog* idea, not a practical plan," she said.

Maybe she was feeling a little better, because for the first time, she sounded like a *cat*.

"It's going to be like a stretcher," Matilda said. "You need to lie on the soft part, and we'll pull it along, and get you to the rescue farm."

"I don't know if it will work," the cat said doubtfully.

The one reliable thing about cats was that they really liked to be *difficult*, especially when it was inconvenient. "If you have a better idea, we're all ears," the Bad Hat said.

She didn't answer for a while, and then she shook her head.

"Are you strong enough to crawl out here, and get on it?" he asked. "Or do you need us to pull you?"

The cat shook her head. "I'll *make* myself strong enough," she said.

It took a long time, and it was hard to watch her move so painfully, but finally, she had dragged herself out from underneath the porch and onto the branches.

"I'm Clarabelle, by the way," she said.

Oh. Right. Because he was such a Bad Hat, he usually forgot about pleasantries. "That's Jack, and MacNulty, and Rachel, and Lancelot, and Matilda, and Duke. And I'm Webster," the dog said. "But, they call me the Bad Hat."

Clarabelle looked at him dubiously. "Do you like that name? It seems unsavory."

Maybe, but he still liked it very much. He nodded. "Yup. We'll try to pull the branch gently, but you need to hang on as best as you can."

He and Duke had just started to pull her down the driveway, when something terrible happened.

The front door of the house opened!

CHAPTER FOURTEEN

H ey!" A lady yelled. She was a large, heavyset woman, who was wearing torn jeans and a stained flannel shirt and looked like she hadn't washed her hair for a week. "Get out of here, you rotten curs!"

Curs?

The Bad Hat didn't realize that she was holding a beer bottle until the lady threw it at them. The bottle hit him right in the side, and he yelped.

"Run," the mother cat gasped. "She'll hurt you. Or her awful husband will come out, and he'll do something even worse. Don't worry, I'll be fine here."

Nope. No way. Not one single, tiny chance in the world. The Bad Hat carefully dropped his end of the branch on the ground so that Clarabelle wouldn't fall off.

"Come on, team," he said. "Let's take care of this varmint!" Then he swaggered up the driveway, with his best cowboy strut, feeling all of the hair on his back rise.

The rest of the dogs were right behind him, although Jack was hopping and Rachel was racing, while MacNulty veered back and forth, and the others moved forward in their breed-specific gaits.

"Get out of here!" the woman yelled, but she sounded a little scared.

Yep. She *should* be afraid.

The Bad Hat kept advancing slowly—ever so slowly, making his eyes as fierce and ominous as possible. He wasn't going to growl, unless he had no choice, but he didn't mind *looking* really scary.

"We can't bite anyone," Duke said urgently. "Biting is bad!"

"We're just *acting* scary," the Bad Hat said.

Duke shook his head. "I don't like it. It seems mean."

The Bad Hat stopped swaggering long enough to stare at him. "You're a *police dog*, man. We're taking control of the scene, to prevent injuries to any innocent bystanders, and then, we'll evacuate the casualty."

Duke's expression relaxed. "Okay. I can do *that*."

So, the dogs kept advancing down the driveway.

"You better not come near me!" the woman said, still cowering on the porch.

The Bad Hat moved even more slowly, never taking his eyes off the woman. Then, he raised his lips, the way Matthew always did, showing her that he had a whole lot of teeth. Big teeth. *Sharp* teeth.

"No biting!" Duke said.

Fine, whatever. "Then, smile at her," the Bad Hat said. "A big, pretty smile that shows all of your teeth."

"Of course," Duke said happily, and beamed at everyone.

The woman hesitated, and the Bad Hat knew that this was the moment when things were either going to get really bad, really fast—or when the woman was going to retreat, like the animal-hating coward that she was.

Maybe ten seconds of utter stillness passed, but it felt like ten hours.

Time to raise the stakes a tiny bit. So, the Bad Hat scraped one paw across the dirt, exactly the way angry bulls did, when they were warning that they were about to charge. Then, he crouched a little, as though he was on the verge of attacking, but he held his position, waiting for the woman's reaction.

"Hey, I could care less what happens to that stupid cat," the lady said gruffly. "Kill it, for all I care. I'm going inside to call Animal Control." She turned around, went—quickly—inside her house, and slammed the door.

The Bad Hat was so relieved that he thought his legs might collapse, but the lady might go inside and get brave—or find a weapon, and there was no time to waste.

"Grab onto the branch with me," he said to MacNulty. "And hang on tight," he said to Clarabelle. "We're getting out of here, as fast as we can."

But, before they even had a chance to take a step, the door flew open again and a burly man with a thick brown beard came lumbering outside.

The Bad Hat's heart sank when he saw that the man was holding a glass bottle in one hand, and a large wooden baseball bat in the other hand.

If the Bad Hat had been by himself, he wouldn't have been worried, because he could easily outrun this guy. But, how were they going to protect a cat who couldn't even sit up all the way, forget run?

"Leave me behind," Clarabelle pleaded. "I'm okay, now that I know my babies are in a good place. I don't mind staying here."

The Bad Hat paid no attention to that. Either they were all going to get away from these awful people—or none of them were.

"Smile at him, Duke," he said. "The biggest smile you have!"

Duke grinned merrily—and the man gasped in fear.

"Keep smiling," the Bad Hat said. "The rest of you, follow me!" He took a deep breath, lowered his head, and charged towards the man full force, with the rest of the dogs only steps behind him.

"Yeah, come get it!" the guy yelled, like some crazy thug from a bad movie.

The Bad Hat knew that he was going to swing the baseball bat at them—and he was prepared for that. Just as the man drew his arm back, the Bad Hat leaped into the air, and caught the handle of the bat in his teeth. He wrenched it out of the guy's hand, and continued right past him. In fact, he had so much momentum, that he actually banged into the side of the house—which hurt. But, he landed effortlessly and spun around to look at the man, still gripping the bat in his teeth.

"Home run!" Jack said, and laughed.

The man threw his beer bottle, and it shattered against the wooden floor of the porch. The Bad Hat instantly closed his eyes, as glass sprayed all around him and—yuck—beer splashed everywhere, too.

"Everyone okay?" he yelled, not opening his eyes yet.

As they all yelled that they were fine, the Bad Hat jumped over the porch railing, with the bat still in his mouth. He landed quite hard on the sparse grass, and then whirled around to face the man, looking as threatening as he knew how to look.

Which was, all things considered, impressively threatening.

The man's eyes widened, as though he was dense enough to think that a dog was actually capable of swinging a baseball bat and doing some damage. Instead, the Bad Hat dropped it, and raced over to the tree branch in the driveway.

"Hang on!" he told the cat. "It's going to be a bumpy ride!"

Clarabelle dug her claws into the branches, gripping

them as well as she could, and the Bad Hat and MacNulty grabbed the end and tugged with all of their might. As they ran down the driveway, dragging the makeshift litter, the man stormed down the front steps. He tried to catch up with them, but Jack and Matilda darted underneath his feet, and the man tripped and fell heavily.

"Keep running!" Matilda yelled, as she squirmed out from underneath the man. "We'll catch up."

"Yeah, hurry!" Jack said. "We'll be right there!"

The Bad Hat and MacNulty didn't hesitate, dragging the branch as quickly as they could, and trying to get as far away from the house as possible.

"What do I do?" Duke asked.

"Just keep smiling, dude," Lancelot said. "And run along with us."

Duke nodded seriously. "Okay. I can do that."

So, the dogs all raced down the driveway, and away from the house.

"Yeah, go!" the man shouted, between raspy coughs. "See if I care!" Then, he hurled the baseball bat after them.

The dogs kept running, and the bat clattered harmlessly onto the ground. The Bad Hat was able to feel from the weight of the branch that Clarabelle was still with them. If the guy started chasing them again, or—worse—got in his stupid truck, and drove after them, it was going to be—no, he couldn't worry about that. He had to concentrate on escaping.

So, he did. They ran up one street, down another, around a corner, and down another street.

When MacNulty saw a path in the woods, he veered to the right and hauled the branch over there. "Come this way!" he yelled.

That was a good idea, so the Bad Hat helped him steer the branch in that direction. That way, they would be out of sight, and could rest for a minute, and maybe have time to stop being terrified.

Clarabelle lay on the branches, gasping, and the Bad Hat and MacNulty leaned against a tree, panting. The rest of the dogs gathered nearby, also panting.

"My mouth is tired," Duke said. "Can I stop smiling for a minute?"

The Bad Hat had to laugh. "Sure. At ease, Duke."

"Whew," Duke said, and let his mouth relax.

"You all right?" the Bad Hat asked Clarabelle, who nodded feebly.

In his opinion, she didn't sound—or look—so good, but okay, he would take her word for it.

"We'll try not to let any people see us," he said, "and we're going to cover you with some leaves, so that if they *do* see anything, we'll just look like some wacky dogs playing with a tree limb."

Clarabelle nodded.

Good. Cats could be pretty cooperative, when they were tired.

Lancelot and Jack and Matilda enthusiastically tore up grass and flowers, and dropped them on Clarabelle, while Rachel gathered some leaves and dropped them on top of her, too.

"Don't suffocate her," MacNulty said. "That's like, a lot of vegetation."

At least, though, it wasn't going to be obvious that they were transporting an ill cat.

It was going to be a long, hot walk to the rescue farm. Their feline passenger was so weak from starvation and thirst, that she even lost consciousness at one point, but there wasn't much they could do about that. Joan and Thomas and Dr. K. would be able to deal with it, the Bad Hat assumed. He hoped so, anyway.

The end of the stick had some sharp splinters that cut into his gums, but he couldn't think of a solution for that, either. He just put one foot in front of the other, and walked with his head down to save energy. Sometimes, he switched off with Duke or Lancelot or Rachel, and MacNulty took a few breaks, too.

Several civilians noticed them, and took the usual cell phone photos, or said things like, "Look, there goes Wandering Webster with some dogs and a big stick!" So far, the leaf camouflage seemed to be working. One woman tried to approach them, but the Bad Hat just stopped and gave her a dead-eyed *don't mess with us* look, and she didn't come any closer.

"You're wicked scary," MacNulty said.

"Yeah, and don't you forget it," the Bad Hat said.

Duke looked worried. "Please smile. It's important that dogs should *always* smile."

Yeah, yeah, yeah. "I'll try," the Bad Hat said. "Want to take a turn with the branch?"

"Certainly," Duke said. "Hang on there, miss," he said to Clarabelle. "We'll be home in no time."

Home. They were going home. It was bizarre to think of it that way, but the Green Meadows Farm was their home. And, yeah, the Bad Hat *liked* it there. He hadn't known that it mattered to have friends, and be involved in their lives, and share things with them, but now, he had learned that it did. In fact, it mattered a lot. Even a notoriously aloof Bad Hat—so famous that he had his own Facebook page and was a media sensation—needed to have companionship. No, he didn't know what was going to happen, or how his life was going to turn out— but, for the first time, he didn't feel dread. He maybe even felt—well—*optimistic.*

Which was completely unfamiliar—but, undeniably *nice.*

"I'm sorry to be so much trouble," Clarabelle whispered.

"Happy to do it, ma'am," the Bad Hat said, in his best cowboy voice. "You just sit tight."

Clarabelle nodded, and let her eyes close again.

The dogs walked slowly, and steadily, down the road, pulling the branch along behind them. One paw, after the other. Clarabelle was pretty heavy, and they had to stop to rest a couple of times. But then, the dogs would get up, and start trudging forward again.

When they got to Green Meadows Farm, they all stopped for a minute, to admire the view.

"It's so pretty," Rachel said happily. "I *love* it here."

"And supper!" Jack said. "We're back just in time for supper."

Which made them all wag their tails.

From where they were standing, the Bad Hat could see that the other rescue dogs were all running around in the meadow.

"You guys should sneak back in there now," he said. "I'll take her the rest of the way."

The dogs looked at each other, and then nodded.

"Okay, Captain," MacNulty said. "See you inside!"

As they ran off, and disappeared around the fence—to wherever the stupid tunnel was, the Bad Hat tried not to think about how exhausted he was. He just focused on bending down, picking up the branch, and making his way to the front door of the house. Then, he eased Clarabelle onto the doormat, and used his right paw to try and brush the leaves off her.

"Are we here?" Clarabelle asked, her voice frail.

The Bad Hat nodded. "Your kittens are inside the house. Everything's going to be okay now."

For the first time, he saw her truly relax, and she sank back onto the welcome mat.

"I don't know how I'll ever thank you," she said.

"Money is good," the Bad Hat said.

Her eyes widened.

"Joke," he said. Then, he barked one sharp bark at the front door.

This time, he heard rapid stumping along the floor inside, and it sounded like Florence got there even before Joan did. But, Joan was the one who opened the door, of course.

"Is that—" Joan turned to shout over her shoulder. "Monica, call Dr. K.! I don't know how he did it, but I think Webster's brought us the mother cat. Thomas, come quickly, you're not going to believe this!"

The Bad Hat stepped off to the side, while Joan tenderly lifted the weak, dehydrated cat into her arms. Thomas came running out from the barn to see what was going on. There was a lot of rapid, excited conversation swirling above him, but the dog was too worn out to pay attention.

He looked up at the doorway, where Florence was smiling at him.

"Well, aren't you a wonder," she meowed.

"I don't know," he barked, and lowered his head bashfully. "Maybe. The others helped a lot."

"There's no maybe about it," Florence said. "I'm so proud of you. All of you!"

When was the last time someone had been genuinely *proud* of him? And *cared* about him? Not since he had been with his mother, and siblings, probably. "I lost my whole family," the dog said. "When I was little. And since then, I've always been alone, and I don't know how to trust anyone, or be nice, and—I'm scared."

Florence nodded. "We all get scared. But, please don't leave again. You belong here, and we love you, and *we're* your family now."

Yes. Maybe they really were. And the dog felt something he hadn't felt since he was tiny.

Happiness. Joy, even! Genuine *joy*.

"So, are you going to come in, and get something to eat and drink?" Florence asked. "Monica is making hamburger to add to everyone's food."

Excellent. "Well, I guess so," he said, and shrugged his very coolest cowboy shrug. "For tonight, anyway. Although I might have to leave again tomorrow. Since I'm a traveling man, by nature. And an icon, and a cowboy, and everything."

Florence smiled. "Okay. Whatever makes you happy,

Webster. We can worry about it in the morning."

Yes, that was a good plan. "So. What are we going to watch tonight?" he asked, as he followed her inside.

"Something fun," Florence promised. "Something *wonderful.*"

Yay!

AUTHOR'S NOTE

Unfortunately, there are millions of stray animals like the Bad Hat and Jack and Florence who need good and loving homes. Please support animal rescue groups and reputable shelters, and consider adopting from one whenever possible. Rescued animals tend to be the most wonderful pets in the world!

There are many ways to help stray animals, including volunteering at your local shelter; adopting a homeless pet; providing needed supplies like clean blankets and beds; and sending donations to help pay for food, veterinary expenses, and the many other costs of maintaining a safe and successful animal shelter.

Here are three charities personally recommended by the Bad Hat and his friends! Any donations these charities receive will be used solely to help animals in need. There are many wonderful rescue groups, located all over the world, so it is very easy to find a way to help animals in your area. But, these three groups are the Bad Hat's favorites.

The Bad Hat Fund

c/o Warm Hearts Humane Society, Inc.

P.O. Box 535

Mt. Ida, AR 71957

warmhearts@earthlink.net

warmheartshumanesociety.com

www.facebook.com/Warmheartshumanesociety

The Jeanne Faucher White Fund

c/o Animal Rescue League of Southern Rhode Island

506B Curtis Corner Road

Peace Dale, RI 02883

www.arlsri.org

The Bad Hat Fund

c/o Riverside Animal Hospital

250 West 108th Street

New York, NY 10025

RiversideAnimalHospital@VETSnyc.com

And remember, please always spay and neuter your pets!

ABOUT THE AUTHOR

Ellen Emerson White grew up in New England and now lives in New York City. She is wicked private.